Dyke Darrel the Railroad Detective; or, The Crime of the Midnight Express

Frank Pinkerton

DYKE DARREL THE RAILROAD DETECTIVE

Or

THE CRIME OF THE MIDNIGHT EXPRESS

By FRANK PINKERTON

1886

CHAPTER I.

A STARTLING CRIME.

"The most audacious crime of my remembrance. "

Dyke Darrel flung down the morning paper, damp from the press, and began pacing the floor.

"What is it, Dyke? " questioned the detective's sister Nell, who at that moment thrust her head into the room.

Nell was a pretty girl of twenty, with midnight hair and eyes, almost in direct contrast with her brother, the famous detective, whose deeds of cunning and daring were the theme of press and people the wide West over.

"An express robbery, " returned Dyke, pausing in front of Nell and holding up the paper.

"I am sorry, " uttered the girl, with a pout. "I shan't have you with me for the week that I promised myself. I am always afraid something will happen every time you go out on the trail of a criminal, Dyke. "

"And something usually DOES happen, " returned the detective, grimly. "My last detective work did not pan out as I expected, but I do not consider that entirely off yet. It may be that the one who murdered Captain Osborne had a hand in this latest crime. "

"An express robbery, you say? "

"And murder. "

"And murder! "

The young girl's cheek blanched.

"Yes. The express messenger on the Central road was murdered last night, and booty to the amount of thirty thousand dollars secured. "

"Terrible! "

1

"Yes, it is a bold piece of work, and will set the detectives on the trail. "

"Did you know the murdered messenger, Dyke? "

"It was Arnold Nicholson. "

"No? "

The girl reeled, and clutched the table at her side for support. The name uttered by her brother was that of a friend of the Barrels, a man of family, and one who had been in the employ of the express company for many years.

No wonder Nell Darrel was shocked at learning the name of the victim.

"You see how it is, Nell? "

"Yes, " returned the girl, recovering her self-possession. "I meant to ask you to forego this man-hunt, but I see that it would be of no use."

"Not the least, Nell, " returned Dyke, with a compression of the lips. "I would hunt these scoundrels down without one cent reward. Nicholson was my friend, and a good one. He helped me once, when to do so was of great inconvenience to himself. It is my duty to see that his cowardly assassins are brought to justice. "

Even as Dyke Darrel uttered the last words a man ran up to the steps and opened the front door.

"I hope I don't intrude, " he said, as he put his face into the room.

"No; you are always welcome, Elliston, " cried Dyke, extending his hand. The new-comer accepted the proffered hand, then turned and smiled on Nell. He was a tall man, with smoothly-cut beard and a tinge of gray in his curling black hair.

Harper Elliston was past thirty, and on the best of terms with Dyke Darrel and his sister, who considered him a very good friend.

2

"You have read the news? " Elliston said, as his keen, black eyes rested on the paper that lay on the table.

"Yes, " returned the detective. "It's a most villainous affair. "

"One of the worst. "

"I was never so shocked, " said Nell. "Do you imagine the robbers will be captured, Mr. Elliston? "

"Certainly, if your brother takes the trail, although I hope he will not."

"Why do you hope so? " questioned Dyke.

"My dear boy, it's dangerous—-"

A low laugh cut short the further speech of Mr. Elliston.

"I supposed you knew me too well, Harper, to imagine that danger ever deterred Dyke Darrel from doing his duty. "

"Of course; but this is a different case. 'Tis said that four men were engaged in the foul work, and that they belong to a league of desperate ruffians, as hard to deal with as ever the James and Younger brothers. Better leave it to the Chicago and St. Louis force, Dyke. I should hate to see you made the victim of these scoundrels. "

Mr. Elliston laid his hand on the detective's arm in a friendly way, and seemed deeply anxious.

"Harper, are you aware that the murdered messenger was my friend? "

"Was he? "

"Certainly. I would be less than human did I refuse to take the trail of his vile assassins. You make me blush when you insinuate that danger should deter me from doing my duty. "

"I am not aware that I said such a thing, " answered Elliston. "I did not mean it if I did. It would please me to have you remain off this trail, however, Dyke. I will see to it that the best Chicago detectives are set to work; that ought to satisfy you. "

"And I sit with my hands folded meantime? "

A look of questioning surprise filled the eyes of Dyke Darrel, as he regarded Mr. Elliston.

"No. But you promised Nell to take her East this spring, to New York-"

"He did, but I forego that pleasure, " cried the girl, quickly. "I realize that Dyke has a duty to perform in Illinois. "

"And so you, too, side with your brother, " cried Mr. Elliston, forcing a laugh. "In that case, I surrender at discretion. "

Dyke picked up and examined the paper once more. "DIED FOR DUTY. BOLD AND BLOODY CRIME AT NIGHT ON THE CENTRAL RAILROAD. "

That was the heading to the article announcing the assassination of the express messenger. The train on which the deed had been committed, had left Chicago at ten in the evening, and at one o'clock, when the train was halted at a station, the deed was discovered. Arnold Nicholson was found with his skull crushed and his body terribly beaten, while, in the bloody hands of the dead, was clutched a tuft of red hair. This went to show that one of the messenger's assailants was a man with florid locks.

Leaving Nell and Mr. Elliston together, Dyke Darrel hastened to the station. He was aware that a train would pass in ten minutes, and he wished to enter Chicago and make an examination for himself. The detective's home was on one of the many roads crossing Illinois, and entering the Garden City—about an hour's ride from the Gotham of the West.

In less than two hours after reading the notice of the crime on the midnight express. Dyke Darrel was in Chicago. He visited the body of the murdered messenger, and made a brief examination. It was at once evident to Darrel, that Nicholson had made a desperate fight for life, but that he had been overpowered by a superior force.

A reward of ten thousand dollars was already offered for the detection and punishment of the outlaws.

"Poor Arnold! " murmured Dyke Darrel, as he gazed at the bruised and battered corpse. "I will not rest until the wicked demons who compassed this foul work meet with punishment! "

There were still several shreds of hair between the fingers of the dead, when Dyke Darrel made his examination, since the body had just arrived from the scene of the murder.

The detective secured several of the hairs, believing they might help him in his future movements. Darrel made one discovery that he did not care to communicate to others; it was a secret that he hoped might lead to results in the future. What the discovery was, will be disclosed in the progress of our story.

Soon after the body of the murdered a messenger was removed to his home, from which the funeral was to take place.

As Dyke Darrel was passing from the rooms of the undertaker, a hand fell on his shoulder.

"You are a detective? "

Dyke Darrel looked into a smooth, boyish face, from which a pair of brown eyes glowed.

"What is it you wish? " Darrel demanded, bluntly.

"I wish to make a confidant of somebody. "

"Well, go on. "

"First tell me if you are a detective. "

"You may call me one. "

"It's about that poor fellow you've just been interviewing, " said the young stranger. "I am Watson Wilkes, and I was on the train, in the next car, when poor Nicholson was murdered. I was acting as brakeman at the time. Do you wish to hear what I can tell? "

CHAPTER II.

DYKE DARREL'S TRICK.

"Certainly I do, " cried the detective. "Come with me, and we will find a place where we can talk without danger of interruption. "

The two men moved swiftly down the street. At length Dyke Darrel entered a well-known restaurant on Randolph street, secured a private stall, and then bade Mr. Wilks proceed. Both men were seated at a small table.

"Shan't I order the wine? "

"No, " answered Dyke, with a frown. "We need clear brains for the work in hand. If you know aught of this monstrous crime, tell it at once. "

"I do know a considerable, " said Mr. Wilks. "I was the first man who discovered Arnold Nicholson after he'd been shot. The safe was in the very car that I occupied. I saw the men get the swag. There were three of them. "

"Go on. "

"They all wore mask, so of course I could not tell who they were; but I've an idea that they were from Chicago. "

"Why have you such an idea? "

"Because I saw three suspicious chaps get on at Twenty-second street. I think they are the chaps who killed poor Arnold, and got away with the money in the safe. "

"Did you recognize them? "

"No—that is, I'm not positive; but I think one of 'm was a chap that is called Skinny Joe, a hard pet, who used to work in a saloon on Clark street. "

"Indeed. "

"Yes. It might be well to keep your eye out in that quarter. "

"It might, " admitted Dyke Darrel. "This is all you know regarding the midnight tragedy? "

"Oh, no; I can give you more particulars. "

"Let's have them, then. "

"But see here, how am I to know that you are a detective? I might get sold, you know, " replied Mr. Wilks in a suspicious tone.

Dyke Darrel lifted the lapel of his coat, exposing a silver star.

"All right, " returned Mr. Wilks, with a nod. "I'm of the opinion that Skinny Joe's about the customer you need to look after, captain. I'll go down with you to the fellow's old haunts, and we'll see what we can find. "

Mr. Wilks seemed tremendously interested. Dyke Darrel was naturally suspicious, and he was not ready to swallow everything his companion said as law and gospel. Of course the large reward was a stimulant for men to be on the lookout for the midnight train robbers; and Mr. Wilks' interest must be attributable to this.

"You see, I was Arnold Nicholson's friend, and I'd go a long ways to see the scoundrels get their deserts who killed him, even if there was no reward in the case, " explained the brakeman suddenly.

"Certainly, " answered Dyke Darrel. "I can understand how one employed on the same train could take the deepest interest in such a sad affair. "

"Will you go down on Clark street with me? "

"Not just now. "

"When? "

"I will meet you here this evening, and consult on that point. "

"Very well. Better take something. "

"No; not now. "

Dyke Barrel rose to his feet and turned to leave the stall.

"Don't fail me now, sir. "

"I will not. "

The detective walked out. The moment he was gone a change came over the countenance of the young brakeman. The pleasant look vanished, and one dark and wicked took its place.

"Go, Dyke Darrel; I am sharp enough to understand you. You distrust me; but you're fooled all the same. It's strange you've forgotten the boy you sent to prison from St. Louis five years ago for passing counterfeit coin. I haven't forgotten it; and, what is more, I mean to get even. "

Then, with a grating of even white teeth, Watson Wilks passed out. At the bar he paused long enough to toss off a glass of brandy, and then he went out upon the street.

It was a raw April day, and the air cut like a knife. After glancing up and down the street Mr. Wilks moved away. On reaching Clark street he hurried along that thoroughfare toward the south. Arriving in a disreputable neighborhood, he entered the side door of a dingy brick building, and stood in the presence of a woman, who sat mending a pair of old slippers by the light afforded by a narrow window.

"Madge Scarlet, I've found you alone, it seems. "

"I'm generally alone, " said the female, not offering to move.

She was past the prime of life, and there were many crow's feet on a face that had once been beautiful. Her dress was plain, and not the neatest. The room was small, and there were few articles of furniture on the uncarpeted floor.

"Madge, where are Nick and Sam? "

"I can't tell you. "

"Haven't they been here to-day? "

"No, not in three days. " "That seems strange. "

"It doesn't to me. They are out working the tramp dodge, in the country, or into some worse iniquity, Watson. I do wish you would quit such company, and try and behave yourself. "

At this the young man gave vent to a sarcastic laugh.

"Now, Aunt Madge, what an idea! Do you suppose your dear nephew could do anything wrong? Aren't I a pattern of perfection? "

Watson Wilks drew himself up and looked as solemn as an owl. This did not serve to bring a pleased expression to the woman's face, however. As she said nothing, the young man proceeded:

"I'm working on the railroad now, Madge, and haven't turned a dishonest penny in a long time. Of course you heard of the robbery of the midnight express down in the central part of the State last night? Some of the morning papers have an account of it. "

"I hadn't heard. "

"Well, then, I will tell you about it; " and Mr. Wilks gave a brief account of the terrible tragedy that had shocked the land. "It's a regular Jesse James affair, and there's a big reward offered for the outlaws. "

The woman seemed interested then, and looked hard at her nephew.

"Watson, I hope you know nothing of this work? "

"Of course I know something of it, " he answered quickly. "I returned in charge of the dead body of the messenger. I was in the next car when he was killed, and one of the robbers put his pistol to my head and threatened to blow my brains out if I said or did anything. You can just bet I kept mighty still. "

"I should think so. This'll make a tremendous stir, " returned the woman. "The country'll be full of man-trackers and it'll go hard with the outlaws if they're captured. "

"You bet; but they won't be captured. " "You are confident? "

"I've a right to be. I—-"

Then the young man ceased to speak suddenly, and his face became deeply suffused.

The woman sprang up then and went to the young man's side, laying her hand on his shoulder.

"Watson, tell me truly that you don't know who committed this crime. "

"Bother! " and he flung her hand from his shoulder with an impatient movement. "I hope you ain't going to turn good all to once, Madge Scarlet. I tell you, thirty thousand dollars ain't to be sneezed at, and I do need money—but of course *I* don't know a thing about who did it, of course not; but I can tell you one thing, old lady, Dyke Barrel is on the trail, and he is even now in Chicago. "

"Dyke Darrel! "

"That's who, Madam. "

For some moments a silence fell over the two that was absolutely painful. At length the woman found her voice.

"Dyke Barrel! Ah! fiend of Missouri, I have good cause to remember you and your work. Do you know, Watson, the fate of your poor uncle? "

"Well, I should smile if I didn't, " answered the young man. "He died in a Missouri dungeon, sent there by this same Dyke Darrel, the railroad man-tracker. Hate him? Of course you do, but not as I do. I have sworn to have revenge for the five years I laid in a dungeon for shoving the queer. "

"And Dyke Darrel is now in Chicago? "

"Yes. I parted from him not an hour since. "

"What is he here for? "

"The crime on the midnight express brings him here. "

"And you saw and talked with him? "

"I did. "

"He recognized you of course? "

"No, he did not; that is the best of it. I am to meet him again to-night. It won't be long before the man who sent Uncle Dan to a Missouri dungeon is in your presence, and you shall do with him as you like, Madge Scarlet. "

"As I like? "

"I have said it. "

"Then Dyke Darrel shall die! "

"That's the talk, " Madge. "THAT sounds like your old self; I am glad you have come to your senses. If Nick and Sam come in, tell them to be in readiness to receive a visitor. "

Then the young man turned on his heel and abruptly left the room. Just as the shades of night were falling Watson Wilks peered into the saloon and restaurant where he had parted from Dyke Darrel earlier in the day.

He saw nothing of the detective.

"It is time he was here, " muttered the young man. "Dyke Darrel is generally prompt in filling engagements. "

"Always prompt, MARTIN SKIDWAY! "

The young villain staggered back against the iron railing near, as though stricken a blow in the face.

Unconsciously he had uttered his thoughts aloud, and the voice that uttered the reply was hissed almost in his ear.

Dyke Darrel stood before him.

The detective's face wore a stern look, which was suddenly discarded for a smile.

"I am prompt in filling engagements, " said Darrel, after a moment. "You see I have at last recognized you, and the walls of the prison from which you escaped shall again envelop you. "

And then a sharp click was heard. The fraudulent brakeman held up his arms helplessly—they were safely secured with handcuffs!

CHAPTER III.

PROFESSOR DARLINGTON RUGGLES.

It would be hard to find a more completely astounded person than the one calling himself Watson Wilks at that moment.

The noted detective had outwitted him completely.

It was humiliating, to say the least.

"This is an outrage! " at length the young villain found voice to utter. "I will call on the police for assistance if you do not at once remove these bracelets. "

"Do so if you like, " answered Dyke Darrel, coolly; so icily in fact as to deter the young man from carrying out his threat. It might be that the detective would delight in turning him over to the Chicago police, a consummation that the fellow dreaded more than aught else.

"Come with me, and make no trouble. You will do so, if you know when you are well off, " said Dyke Darrel significantly.

And Wilks walked along peacefully, allowing the sleeves of his coat to hide the handcuffs. After going a few blocks, the detective hailed a hack, and pushing his prisoner before him, entered and ordered the driver to make all speed for the Union depot.

"What does this mean? " demanded the prisoner, with assumed indignation.

"It means that you will take a trip South for your health, my friend. "

"To St. Louis? "

"You have guessed it, Skidway. "

A troubled look touched the face of the escaped prisoner.

"Why do you call me by that name, Dyke Darrel? "

"Because that IS your name. You have five years unexpired term yet to serve in the Missouri penitentiary, and I conceive it my duty to see that you keep the contract. "

"A contract necessarily requires two parties. I never agreed to serve the State. "

"Well, we won't argue the point. "

"But I am in the employ of the railroad company, and will lose my place—-"

"You gain another one, so it doesn't matter, " retorted the detective. "No use making a fuss, Mr. Skidway; you cannot evade the punishment which awaits you. Any confession you choose to make I am willing to hear. The late tragedy, for instance? "

"You'll get nothing out of me. "

"I am sorry, "

"Of course you are. Did you recognize me when we first met? "

"No. It was an afterthought. "

"I thought so. You shall suffer for this. You've got the wrong man, Mr. Darrel. "

"You seem to know me. "

"Everybody does. "

"You flatter me. "

"My name isn't Skidway, but Wilks, and I can prove it. "

"Do so. "

"Release me and I will. "

"I'm not that green. "

The prisoner muttered angrily. He realized that he was fairly caught, and that it was too late now to think of deceiving the famous detective.

Dyke Darrel had recognized in the young man calling himself Watson Wilks an old offender, who had made his escape from the Missouri State prison three months before, and he at once surmised that the young counterfeiter, who was a hard case, might have had a hand in the murder and robbery of the express messenger. Reasoning thus, the detective decided upon promptly arresting the fellow before proceeding to search further. It would be safer to have Skidway in prison than at large in any event.

More than one pair of eyes had watched the departure of Dyke Darrel and his prisoner from Chicago, and a little later a bearded man, with deep-set, twinkling eyes, and the general look of a hard pet, thrust his head into Madge Scarlet's little room, and said:

"It are all up with the kid, Mrs. Scarlet. "

"What's that you say? "

The woman came to her feet and confronted the new-comer with an interested look.

"It's all up with the kid. "

"Come in, Nick Brower, and let me have a look at your face. I want no lies now, " cried the woman sharply; and the man drew himself into a little room, and stood regarding the female with a grin.

"Now let me hear what you've got to tell, " demanded Mrs. Scarlet.

"It's ther kid—"

"Watson? "

"Yesum. "

"Well, what has happened to him, man? Can't you speak? "

"He's took. "

"Took? "

"Nabbed. Got the darbies on and gone South a wisitin'. "

"Do you mean to say that Watson has been arrested? "

"I do, mam, " grunted Brower. "He's well out of town, goin' South, and I reckin he'll be in Jeffe'son City before we hear from him agin. I seed him a-goin' with my own eyes. "

"How did it happen? "

The man explained how young Skidway had been seized and taken on board the train by Dyke Darrel.

"You are sure his captor was Dyke Darrel? "

"I ain't blind, I reckon, " growled the man. "I heard sufficient to tell me that the detective was takin' the kid back to Missoury, and that was enough for me. "

"Why did you permit it? "

A laugh answered the woman.

"You might have saved the boy, " pursued Mrs. Scarlet, angrily. "Now he will spend another five years in the dungeon where my poor man died of a broken heart. Watson told me that the infamous Dyke Darrel was in Chicago; but I had no thought of his recognizing the boy. Can you lend me some money, Nick? "

"A purty question, Madge. Don't you know I'm always dead-broke? " growled Brower. "What in the nation do you want with money any how? "

"I'm going to St. Louis. "

"No? "

"I am. If Dyke Darrel puts my boy behind prison bars again, I will have no mercy. It's life for life. I am tired of living, and am willing to die to revenge myself on that miserable detective. "

16

Mrs. Scarlet began pacing the room. She was deeply moved, and tears of anger and sorrow glittered in her eyes. She was about to utter a fierce tirade against the detective, when a step sounded without, followed immediately by three raps on the door.

"Whist! " exclaimed Brower. "It is the Professor. "

Madge Scarlet crossed the floor and admitted a visitor, a tall man with fire-red hair and beard, who was well clad and wore blue glasses. A plug hat, rather the worse for wear, was lifted and caressed tenderly with one arm as the gentleman bowed before Mrs. Scarlet.

"I am pleased to find you at home, Mrs. Scarlet. "

"I seldom go out, Mr. Ruggles, or Professor Darlington Ruggles, I suppose. "

"Never mind the handle, madam. I see you have company. " The Professor turned a keen glance on Nick Brower as he spoke.

CHAPTER IV.

SCALPED.

The gentleman is a friend, " said Mrs. Scarlet. "You need not fear to speak before him. "

"I hain't no wish to hear any private talk, " said Nick Brower, and with that he cast a keen, knowing look into the visitor's face, and passed from the room.

"We're alone, Professor. "

"So it seems. "

"What news do you bring? "

"Have you heard of the midnight express robbery? "

"I have. "

"And that Dyke Darrel is on the trail? "

"I have heard all that, and more, " said the woman. "My nephew has been arrested and taken to Missouri by this same infamous Dyke Darrel. It was an awful blow to me; it leaves me entirely alone in the world. I am ready to do anything to compass the ruin of the detective who brought me to this. "

"I am glad to hear you say it, madam. I came here for advice and help. I assure you that it is highly necessary for all of us that Dyke Darrel be removed. "

"Well? "

"He might be enticed here, and quietly disposed of. "

"Will you entice him? "

"I might; but —-"

"Well? " as the man hesitated.

"You see, I've got a place to fill in the world, and don't want to mix with anything that's unlawful, " and the Professor stroked his red beard in a solemn manner.

"Yet you would be glad to see Dyke Darrel dead? "

"Hush, woman! Walls have ears. You are imprudent. I have nothing against Mr. Darrel in particular, only he has injured my friends, and may be up to more of his tricks. Now, as regards Watson Wilks, you say Dyke Darrel has gone to Missouri with the boy in charge? "

"Yes. The last friend I had in the world has been torn from me, to languish in prison. I will have the detective's heart's blood for this, " cried the woman, with passionate vehemence.

"Of course, " agreed the Professor. "But of what crime was the young man accused? Not the one on the midnight express, I hope? " The tall visitor bent eagerly forward then, and penetrated the woman with a keen gaze.

"No, no, " was the quick reply. "I know that Martin had no hand in that. "

"Martin? "

"Watson, I mean, " corrected Mrs. Scarlet. "I sometimes call the boy Martin, which is his middle name, so he has a right to it. "

"Exactly. You KNOW that the boy had nothing to do with the robbery last night. I don't wish to argue or dispute with a lady, but I shall be compelled to question HOW you know so much. Will you answer? "

"Because—because Martin is incapable of such work. I have read all about it in the papers, and am confident that it was the work of an organized band. " The Professor laughed until his white teeth gleamed in the lamplight.

"So sure! " he said. "You consider that nephew of yours a pattern of propriety. Is this the only reason you have for believing that Watson Wilks had no hand in the murder of Arnold Nicholson, and the rifling of the express company's safe? "

"I have another! "

"Well? "

"He was in Chicago at the time the deed was done. "

"Can you prove this? "

Professor Ruggles seemed extremely eager, as he bent forward and touched the arm of Madge Scarlet with a white forefinger.

"I can prove it. "

"Very good. It may never be necessary, but if the worst comes, you may be called on. I suppose you're not in the best of circumstances, Mrs. Scarlet? "

The Professor drew forth his wallet. "I shall suffer, now that my boy is gone. "

"Don't fear that, madam, " returned Darlington Ruggles, as he laid a bank note for a large amount in her hand. Providence and your friends will take care of you. You have rendered me more than one good service, and I may call on you for more, soon, much sooner than you imagine. "

"Anything I can do, Professor, will be gladly performed; " was the woman's answer, as she clutched the bank note eagerly, and thrust it from sight.

Then Professor Ruggles turned to the door. Here he paused and faced the woman once more.

"Madge, what charge was your nephew arrested under? "

"An old one. "

"That is not an answer, " and the man frowned.

"The charge is for uttering counterfeit coin. I believe the boy was innocent, but there was money on the other side, and Martin was sent up for ten years; my husband for fifteen. My man died of a broken heart, being innocent, and Martin served five years and then escaped. "

"I understand. I don't think the boy will ever serve out his time. "

"I hope he may not, but—-"

"Keep a stout heart, Mrs. Scarlet. Influences are at work to free the boy. It will not do to permit him to languish in prison. I tell you Providence is on your side. "

Then Mr. Darlington Ruggles passed from the room.

"Strange man, " muttered the woman, after he had gone. "He is a mystery. Sometimes I imagine he is not what he seems, but a detective. I hope I have given nothing away, for I find it won't do to trust anybody these days. "

In the meantime Professor Darlington Ruggles made his way to another part of the city, not far from the river, and met a man in a dingy basement room at the rear of a low doggery.

Strange place for a learned professor, was it not?

"You've kept me waiting awhile, boss. "

The speaker was the man we have seen at Madge Scarlet's—Nick Brower by name.

"I couldn't get away sooner, " returned the professor. "How does the land lay, Nat? "

"In an ugly quarter. "

"I feared so myself. The young chap that Dyke Darrel took to Missouri knows enough to hang you—-"

"And you, too, pard; don't forget that, " retorted the grizzled villain grimly.

"I forget nothing, " said Mr. Ruggles, giving his plug hat a rub across his left arm. "It isn't pleasant, to say the least, having matters turn out in this way. I wish to see you in regard to this Dyke Darrel. "

"I'm all ears, pard. "

"He must never see Chicago again. "

"Wal? " "I want you to see to it, Nick. "

"I don't know about that, " muttered the grosser villain. "I've shed 'bout enough blood, I reckin. "

"It is for your own safety that I speak, Nick. No trace of that last work can ever reach me. "

"Don't be too sure, Darl Ruggles. With Dyke Darrel on the trail, there's no knowing where it'll end. He's unearthed some o' the darkest work ever did in Chicago an' St. Louis. I WOULD breathe a durn sight more comfortable like if Dyke Darrel was under the sod. "

"So would others. "

"Yourself, fur instance. "

"I won't deny it, Nick. I don't feel very comfortable with the young detective free. Between you and me, Nick, I believe we can make this the last trail Dyke Darrel ever follows. A thousand dollars to the man who takes the detective's scalp. That is worth winning, Nick. "

"Put 'er thar, pard. "

Nick Brower held out his huge hand and clasped the small white one of the Professor.

"I'll win that thousan' or go beggin' the rest o' my days, Darl Ruggles. "

"I hope you may. You'd best take the next train for the Southwest. I won't be far behind. "

And then the two separated.

A little later Professor Darlington Ruggles stood on the dock overlooking the river and the shipping. Although yet early in the season the big lake was open, and several vessels laden with lumber had entered the river from various ports on the Eastern shore during the day.

A tug lay on the further side, and a schooner with bare spars loomed up in the moonlight.

"This open sewer has witnessed more thar one crime, " mused the Professor. "I would like it if that infernal Dyke Darrel was at the bottom of the river. He has taken into his head to hunt down the men who killed Arnold Nicholson, and if there's a man east of the Mississippi who can ferret out this crime, Dyke Darrel is the one. But I don't mean to permit him to do anything of the kind if I know myself. It's a fight between the detective and as sharp a man as any detective that ever lived. I imagine—hello! who is this? "

The last exclamation was caused by the sudden appearance of a dark form coming up over the dock as if from the water. A moment later a man paused within six feet of Professor Ruggles, and penetrated him with a pair of glittering eyes.

"What do you want? "

It was the Professor who uttered the word, at the same time receding a step or two, for the stranger's glance startled him considerably.

"Who are you? " demanded the stranger, shortly.

"It does not concern you. "

"Don't it? We'll see about that. "

An arm shot forward. The Professor's plug fell to the ground, and the next instant a red wig was swung aloft in the moonlight.

"Ha! I thought so. You are the man I seek—"

The speaker's words were cut off suddenly.

CHAPTER V.

ELLISTON'S REBUFF.

A mad cry fell from the lips of the Professor when he felt himself unceremoniously scalped. The next instant his right hand drew forth a gleaming knife.

"Oh! Ah! MURDER! "

A dark form went backward over the dock; a splash followed, and the Professor stood alone. He peered into the muddy water to note the fact that it flowed on calmly as before.

Then Ruggles picked up his hat and wig, and readjusted them on his head.

"My soul! that was a narrow escape. "

At this moment another form was seen approaching, and the Professor, deeming it prudent to move away, was soon striding from the spot, his tall form disappearing in the shadows before the third person reached the edge of the dock.

****

On the day following the events last narrated, a man ran up the steps at the Darrel cottage in Woodburg, and rang the bell.

Nell answered, and met the gentlemanly Mr. Elliston. She led the way at once to a room opening from the hall, where preparations had been made for a lunch.

"Where is Dyke? " questioned the gentleman the moment he was seated.

"I haven't seen him since he left for Chicago to look into the express robbery, " returned Nell. "Haven't you met him? "

"No. Strange he did not write if he meant to be gone long, " remarked Elliston. "You were about to dine, I see. "

"Yes; will you keep me company? "

"With pleasure. "

"I thought Dyke would be with me ere this, " proceeded Nell, as they discussed the edibles. "When he goes for a long stay she usually drops me a line. "

After the lunch, Mr. Elliston left his chair and crossed the room to glance from the window, at the same time plucking at his short beard in an apparently nervous manner.

Nell was on the point of removing the ware from the table, when Mr. Elliston turned suddenly, and resumed his seat at the table.

"Sit down, Nell, I wish a word with you. "

The girl sank once more into a chair, wondering what was coming.

Laying both hands on her shoulders, Harper Elliston looked her in the eyes and said:

"You must have guessed the object of my visit to-day, Nellie Darrel."

She blushed under his gaze, and looked away nervously.

"N—oo, I can't say that I do. I suppose you came to see my brother. "

"Not so. It is you I wished to see, Nell. Why have I come here so often? I know you must have guessed before this. I love you, dear girl, and want you to be mine—"

He could say no more then, for Nell Darrel started sharply to her feet, pressing her hands to her burning face.

"No, no, not that. " she murmured. "I never suspected that, Mr. Elliston. "

"But listen to me, Nell, " he pleaded, reaching up and attempting to draw her hands aside. "I can give you a handsome home in New York. If you will be my wife, I will return there at once. "

She tore herself from his hands, and her confusion vanished, a feeling of indignation taking its place.

"Mr. Elliston, I tell you I do not love you, and never can. I was never more surprised in my life than now. You are old enough to be my father, sir. "

He came to his feet also, and leaned with his hands clinching the top of a chair. There was a frown on his brow and a glitter in his black eyes unpleasant to see.

"Must I call you coquette? " he said, in an undertone of concentrated feeling. "You certainly have encouraged me. "

"Never, sir, " was the indignant response.

"Then our paths must lie apart hereafter, I suppose, Miss Darrel? "

"That is as you shall determine, " she answered. "As my brother's friend, I have tolerated you, and can do so in the future. "

"Ah! It was only TOLERATION then. I did not think this of you, Nell Darrel. Do you know that many of the wealthiest, most beautiful maidens of Gotham would jump at the offer you have just spurned so lightly? "

"I will not deny it. "

"I could have long ago taken a partner to share my life in my elegant home on Fifth avenue, but do you know the reason of my not doing so? I can tell you. I had not seen a girl to my taste. Until I came West I believed I should never marry. From the moment of meeting you, however, I changed my mind. To see was to love, and —"

"Please cease, Mr. Elliston, " pleaded Nell Darrel, putting out her hand deprecatingly. "This is a most painful subject to me. "

"Very well. "

With a sigh he crossed the floor and stood by the window once more. He seemed struggling to keep down his emotions. At that moment the detective's sister pitied the man, and felt really sorry that she had unintentionally been the means of making him miserable.

"Mr. Elliston, please do not feel so badly. I respect you, and hope we may ever be friends. "

She approached him and held out her hand. He turned and regarded her with a queer glow in his eyes.

"I accept your proffer of continued friendship, " he said with a forced smile. "It is better so than open war between us. "

"It would avail nothing to make war on a friend, " she said simply. "I respect you very highly, Mr. Elliston, and as Dyke's friend, shall always hope to retain your good opinion. "

"Whatever may happen, you will have that, " he returned.

Soon after the gentleman departed. The moment he was gone Nell Darrel sank to a chair, and, bowing her head on the table, began to cry.

Strange proceeding, was it not, after what had taken place? Women are enigmas that man, after ages of study, has been unable to solve.

Another face came before the girl's mind at that moment, the face of one to whom her heart had been given in the past, and who, for some unaccountable reason, had failed to put in an appearance or write during the past six months.

"If Harry were only here, " murmured the girl, as she raised her head and wiped the tears from her pretty eyes. "I know something has happened to him—something terrible. "

At this moment Aunt Jule, the colored housekeeper, the only other resident of the cottage, aside from Nell Barrel and her brother, entered the room, and her appearance at once put an end to Nell's weeping.

"Marse Elliston done gone. What did he want, honey? "

"To see Dyke, " answered Nell, with a slight twinge at uttering such a monstrous falsehood.

"Marse Dyke don't come yet. 'Deed but he's full of business dese times. Marse Dyke a great man, honey. "

If the old negress noticed traces of tears on the face of her young mistress, she was sharp enough to keep the discovery to herself.

In the meantime, Mr. Elliston made his way to the principal hotel in the little city and sought his room. He was a regular boarder, but, like other men of leisure, he was not regular at meals or room. Nevertheless, he paid his board promptly, and that was the desideratum with the landlord.

The man's teeth gleamed above his short, gray-streaked beard, as he sat down and meditated on the situation.

"So, I can be her friend still. Well, that is something. I don't mean to give up so. Dark clouds are gathering over your life, Nell Darrel, and when the blackest shadow of the storm bends above and howls about you, in that hour you may conclude that even an elderly gentleman like myself will DO. "

Again the man's teeth gleamed and the black eyes glittered.

"I have set my heart on winning that girl. A mock marriage will do as well as anything, and such beauty and freshness will bring money in New York. "

Harper Elliston remained in his room until a late lour. After the shades of evening fell he left the room and hotel with a small grip in his hand. He turned his steps in the direction of the railway station. Arrived at the depot, he purchased a ticket for St. Louis. Then he sauntered outside and stood leaning against the depot in a shaded spot.

It would be five minutes only until the departure of the train. There were troubled thoughts in the brain of Harper Elliston that night.

A touch on his hand caused him to start. At thin fold of paper was passed into his palm. Turning quickly, Elliston saw a shadowy form disappear in the gloom.

"Confound it, who are you? " growled the tall man, angrily. Then, remembering the paper, he went to a light, and opening it, held it up to his gaze.

"HARPER ELLISTON: Go slow in your plot against Nell Darrel. She has a friend who will see that her enemies are punished. Beware! The volcano on which you tread is about to burst. "

No name was signed to the paper.

At this moment the express came thundering in; the conductor's "all aboard" sounded, and, crunching the paper in his hands, Elliston had hardly time to spring on board ere the train went rushing away into the darkness.

CHAPTER VI.

DYKE DARREL'S DANGER.

Martin Skidway was an old offender, and through the efforts of Dyke Darrel he and his uncle had been detected in crime and sent to the Missouri State prison for a term of years. It was a mere accident that the detective came upon the escaped young counterfeiter, or rather it was through the young villain's own foolhardiness that he was again in durance vile.

"I will not serve my time out, you can bet high on that, " asserted the young prisoner in a confident tone.

Dyke Darrel more than half suspected that the young counterfeiter knew something of the late crime on the midnight express, and during the ride to St. Louis he did all that he could to worm a confession from the prisoner.

"It is possible that you may get your freedom at an early day, " said the detective. "I have heard of men turning State's evidence, and profiting by it. "

"I suppose so. "

"I would advise you to think on this, Martin Skidway. "

"Why should I think on it? Do you think I'm a fool, Dyke Darrel? "

"Not quite, " and the detective smiled. "I know you have been pretty sharp, young man, but not keen enough to escape punishment. You have five years yet to serve, at the end of which time you may be arrested and hung for another crime. "

"You are giving me wind now. "

"I am not. A terrible crime was committed four and twenty hours since, and on this road; a midnight crime that the whole country will work to punish. It will we impossible for the express robbers to escape. "

"You are a braggart! "

30

"I do not say that *I* will be the one to bring these villains to justice, but I do say that justice will be done, and I expect to see the murderers of Arnold Nicholson hung. " The keen eyes of Dyke Darrel fixed themselves on the face of his prisoner, with a penetrating sharpness that fairly made the fellow squirm in his seat. On more than one occasion had the railroad detective brought confession from the lips of guilt, through the magnetism of his terrible glance.

He tried his powers on the man at his side, and found him yielding to the pressure, when Skidway suddenly turned his face to the window, and refused to encounter the gaze of his captor.

By this means he was able to defy the magnetic powers of the detective.

"Martin Skidway, you may as well admit that you know something of this latest villainy. Even if you were not connected with it, you know WHO was? "

The prisoner remained silent.

Dyke Darrel proceeded:

"You said that you were a brakeman on the train on which poor Nicholson found his death. Was that the truth? "

"It was. "

"It is now for your own good that you make confession, Martin Skidway! "

"I've nothing to confess. "

"Be careful! "

"You can't scare me into telling a lie, " said the prisoner, with an assumption of bravado that he did not feel. "I don't know anything about the express robbers, only what I've told you; you can make the most of that. "

"I mean to do so, " assured Dyke Darrel. "I shall not leave the trail until the perpetrators of that crime are secured and punished. In that day you may wish that you had not been so obstinate. "

"I have told all I know. "

"I hope you have! "

"You believe I am lying, Dyke Darrel? "

"It doesn't matter what I believe, " retorted the detective. "Of course, you are not of the sort who believe in telling facts when a falsehood will serve you better. I did not expect anything different. "

Arrived at the Southwestern metropolis, Dyke Darrel turned his prisoner over to the proper officers, warning them of the dangerous nature of young Skidway, and then he turned his thoughts and feet in another channel.

Dyke Darrel went to the office of the railroad company on whose road the midnight crime had been committed, and consulted with one of the officers in regard to the same.

CHAPTER VI

DYKE DARREL'S DANGER.

"It is a terrible affair, " said Mr. Holden, the officer in question. "I telegraphed our folks in Chicago to employ detectives in that city, and expect to have the best talent in the country look into this. "

"Of course. Any clew discovered? "

"None. "

"I believe the villains covered their tracks well, " said Dyke Darrel. "The express messenger who was murdered was a personal friend. "

"Your friend? "

"Yes; one I had known for years, which explains my interest in the case. I suppose I have your good wishes in hunting down the outlaws? "

"Well, of course; but it is a task that may tax the coolness and ingenuity of skilled detectives. Amateurs have no place on this case, I assure you. "

"Admitted, " returned the young detective, with a smile. "You have heard of Dyke Darrel? "

"I should think I had. He is the best detective in the West, now that Pinkerton is gone; he was a trusted friend of Allan Pinkerton, too. "

"He was. "

"I've telegraphed for our people to see about employing Dyke Darrel. I shan't be content without. "

Again a smile swept the face of the young detective.

"It seems that you never met Dyke Darrel, Mr. Holden. "

"Never; but—-"

"You see him now at any rate. "

"What? "

"*I* am Dyke Darrel. "

"YOU? "

"The same. "

"Dyke Darrel, the railroad detective; the fellow who captured the brute Crogan, and broke up the counterfeiters' nest near Iron Mountain; the man who has sent more criminals over the road than any other detective in the wide West—YOU? "

"The same, at your service, " and Darrel bowed and smiled again.

"Well, I AM astonished. "

Nevertheless the incredulous railway official seemed pleased at the last, and shook the young detective warmly by the hand.

"I am glad to meet you, Mr. Darrel, and hope we can induce you to take up this case. A great many suspects have been reported, but I take stock in none of them. I trust the whole affair (the management of it, I mean) to you. Will you go into it, Mr. Darrel? "

"Certainly. "

Some time longer the detective and official talked, and the lamps in the streets were lit when Dyke Darrel left the presence of Mr. Holden, and turned his steps toward a hotel.

"I must send a line to Nell, " mused the detective, as he moved along. "I shall remain a short time in St. Louis, as I may pick up some points here that will be of use to me. I am of the opinion that either this city or Chicago holds the perpetrators of this latest railroad crime. "

The detective did not see the shadowy form flitting along not far behind. A man had shadowed the detective since his departure from the railway office. Dyke Darrel, in order to make a short cut, had entered a narrow street, where the lights were few and the buildings dingy and of a mean order.

Moving on, deeply wrapped in thought, the detective permitted his "shadow" to steal upon him, and just as Dyke Darrel came opposite a narrow alley, the shadow sprang forward and dealt him a stunning blow on the head.

The detective reeled, but did not fall. Partially stunned, he turned upon his assailant, only to meet the gleam of cold steel as a knife descended into his bosom!

CHAPTER VII.

WHAT A HANDKERCHIEF REVEALED.

Dyke Darrel was so dazed from the blow he had received as to be unable to ward off the dirk that was thrust at his bosom by the vile assassin, and had not a third party appeared on the scene at this critical moment the story we are now writing would never have been told.

A kind Providence had on more than one occasion favored the daring railroad detective.

Before the point of the knife touched the breast of Dyke Darrel, a swift-flying object sent the deadly weapon out into the middle of the street.

The next instant a man bounded from the shadow of a building upon the would-be assassin. There was a short struggle, when the last comer found, that instead of the detective's assailant, he held a coat in his hands.

The villain had made good his escape.

"Confound you! " greeted the new comer.

"Who was it? "

"I saw him following you, sir, and made up my mind that some villainy was in the wind. I do not know who the villain was. Are you hurt? "

"Not in the least. "

Then the two men walked on until a lamp-post was gained. Here the features of each were plainly revealed.

A low exclamation fell from the lips of Dyke Darrel.

"Good thunder, Harry Bernard! how are you? Where in the world did you spring from? "

The detective grasped and wrung the man's hand warmly—a rather slender young fellow, with brown hair and eyes, a mustache being the only sign of beard on his face.

"One question at a time, Dyke, " returned the young man with a laugh. "I mistrusted it was you all the time. It strikes me that you are becoming careless in your old age. Hope you're not in love—THAT makes a fool of a man sometimes? "

"Does it? No, I'm not in any such predicament; fact is, I am wedded to my profession and shall never marry. But, Harry, you haven't answered my questions yet. "

"You asked me how I get on; I can answer that by saying that I was never better in my life. I have been across the plains, among cowboys and Indians, and it's given me strong muscles and good health. I arrived in St. Louis this morning. It was the merest chance that placed me in a position to do you a service, Dyke. As I said before, it seems to me that you are getting careless. Just imagine what the result would have been had I not put in an appearance. I have the fellow's coat to show for the adventure. "

"True enough. I admit that I was careless, " returned the detective, "and my adventure will serve to put me on my guard hereafter. Come with me to my room, Harry, and we will talk over matters in general. I must take the midnight express North, and may not see you again soon, unless you conclude to go on with me. "

"I shall remain in St. Louis for the present, " returned young Bernard.

He went with his friend to the hotel, however, and soon the two were in the privacy of Dyke Darrel's room.

"Now, then, let us look at that coat. " Harry Bernard laid the garment down on the bed, and Darrel began a close examination of the same. It was an ordinary sack coat, with two inside pockets. The detective was not long in going through the pockets.

"Ah! "

The ejaculation was significant.

It fell from the lips of Dyke Darrel, the detective.

"Now what? " questioned Bernard.

"Look at that. "

Dyke Darrel held aloft a handkerchief that had once been white, but which was now dingy with dirt. But this was not the only discoloration. There was a stain on the square bit of linen that was significant.

"What is it? "

"Blood! " answered Dyke Darrel.

Then the detective made a close examination, and made still another discovery—a name in one corner of the rumpled handkerchief.

The keen eyes of the detective gleamed with a satisfied light.

"What have you discovered, Dyke? "

"A clew. "

"To what? "

"To the most infamous crime of the century. This handkerchief has the name of its owner stamped plainly in the corner. "

"Well? "

"Arnold Nicholson. "

"What? "

"That is the name on this bit of linen, which shows that it was once the property of the murdered express messenger. Of course you have heard of the crime on the Central? "

"Yes. It gave me a shock, too. Arnold was a good fellow. "

Harry Bernard's face wore a serious look as he took the blood-stained handkerchief from the hand of the detective, and examined it with mournful interest.

"It must be that you were assaulted by one of the train robbers, Dyke, " said the youth, as he returned the relic of that midnight crime.

"I imagine so. The scoundrels have discovered that I am on the trail, and they mean to put me out on the first base, if possible. Did you see the man's face who assaulted me, Harry? "

"Imperfectly. I know, however, that he had red hair. "

"Ah! "

"You suspected as much? "

"Yes. In the dead man's fingers was a bit of red hair. It seems conclusive that the villain who assaulted me to-night was the one who engaged in the death struggle with poor Nicholson. The trail is becoming plain, and before the National holiday rolls round I hope to have the perpetrator of this crime behind prison bars. "

"I hope you are not over-sanguine, Dyke. "

"I have ever been successful. "

"How about the Osborne case? "

"Ah, yes; but that isn't off yet. I expect that the murderers of the old captain will come to light about the time the railway criminals are brought to justice. "

"Indeed. "

"There are several hands engaged in these bloody crimes, and when I do make a haul, it will be a wholesale one. "

"I should think you would need help in a work of this kind. "

"I do. "

"Can I be of any service? You may command me, Dyke. "

"Thanks. You were of inestimable service to-night, and I believe you can do more. It would please me to have you remain in this city and keep an eye out, while I go up the road to the spot where the crime was committed. "

"You know the place? "

"Certainly. It was near Black Hollow, a wild spot, where the woods along the creek afforded chance for hiding. Some of the rascals are yet in that vicinity, I believe. The one who assaulted me to-night may not remain in the city long. You will do as I wish? "

"Certainly; glad to do it, Dyke. "

"That settles one point, then. If I need any more help I know where I can find it. "

"Where? "

"Elliston. He is something of a detective, you know. "

Harry Bernard frowned at mention of that name. The pleasant look vanished from his face, and he relapsed into silence.

Holding up the handkerchief, Dyke Darrel said:

"This was used by the assassin to wipe his bloody hands after the murder. He was a fool to keep the tell-tale linen by him; but these fellows are always leaving some loophole open. I have made one discovery that may have escaped your notice, Harry. "

"What is that? "

"Look. " Laying the bloody handkerchief over the young man's knee, Dyke Darrel pointed to a spot near the center, where the imprint of fingers was plainly visible.

"You see that? "

"Certainly; the marks of human fingers, but I can't see that you will be able to make anything out of that, so many hands are alike, you know. "

Then Harry laid his own hand against the spot stained with blood. "My hand fits exactly. "

The eyes of Dyke Darrel began to dilate. His usually immobile features began to twitch, and a deadly pallor overspread all.

What was it that had caught the eye of Dyke Darrel, to cause such terrible emotion? He had indeed made a discovery.

A close examination of the finger-marks showed a white circle, centered with a ragged dot of blood near the knuckle; this had undoubtedly been caused by a wart on the hand of the assassin. It was this fact that had attracted and interested Dyke Darrel, and what he intended showing his friend Harry Bernard. The moment Harry laid his hand against the print on the handkerchief the detective made a startling discovery. Not only did the hand of Harry Bernard fit the bloody stain exactly, but a large wart near the knuckle of the little finger fell exactly against the spot that dotted the center of the white circle.

A feeling of unutterable horror filled the mind of Dyke Darrel at that moment. Harry Bernard had been his friend for years, and he had always found him upright and true.

But what meant this horrible revelation of the handkerchief?

Could it be possible that another had the same-sized hand and a wart near the knuckle of the little finger? It was not likely.

Dyke Darrel came to his feet, with cold perspiration oozing out upon his brow. Before him sat Harry Bernard, smiling gently, and yet he had a devil in his heart—THE DEVIL OF ASSASSINATION!

CHAPTER VIII.

A PLUNGE TO DEATH.

For some moments neither man spoke. Harry Bernard noticed that his friend was deeply moved, and he seemed to wonder at the cause. At length he said:

"Dyke, what is it? "

"Nothing, only —-"

"Well, speak out, " as the detective hesitated.

"It is strange that your hand should so exactly fit the marks on the handkerchief, Harry. "

"Well, yes, " admitted the youth; "I hope you didn't imagine, however, that *I* had a hand in this railway robbery and murder? "

At the last Harry Bernard laughed lightly. Dyke Darrel did not seem to relish the young fellow's lightness, and only frowned.

"This is not a laughing matter, Harry Bernard, " said the detective, sternly.

"Well I should say not. If you have a serious thought that I could do such a deed, Dyke, place me under arrest at once. "

There was an expression of rebuke on the face of Bernard as he uttered the last words. He did not look like a criminal, that was certain, and after a moment Dyke Darrel felt ashamed of his suspicions.

"Never mind, Harry, I could not help feeling shocked. Let it pass; I will not wrong you by suspicion. But you will admit that it was a strange thing, your hand fitting so perfectly. "

"Not at all. Put your own hand here, " returned Bernard.

Dyke Darrel did so, but it was not so near a fit as Harry's. It was not the size of the hand, but the imprint of the wart that had so startled the detective. Harry had not discovered the true cause of his friend's excitement, and the detective concluded to say nothing about it then.

Time was flying. The midnight express would soon leave the city.

"I cannot remain with you longer, " said Dyke Darrel, at length. "I shall leave the case at this end of the route in your hands, Harry, and if at any time you wish to communicate with me, address me at Woodburg. "

"All right. What shall we do with this? "

Harry indicated the coat that still lay on the bed.

"You may retain that, but I will keep the handkerchief. Both may be of use in the future. "

Soon after the two men separated.

Dyke Darrel went at once to the depot, and soon after nine that evening he was speeding northward at the rate of forty miles an hour. At the first stop outside of the city three passengers boarded the train. One was a short, thick-set man, with beard and hair of a dark color; the others were women. The man entered the smoking car and thrust himself into an unoccupied seat, and glanced keenly about him.

The man had no ticket, but paid the conductor to a station a hundred miles from the city.

While sitting with his back to the aisle, a touch on the shoulder roused him.

"Eh, it's you, Ruggles? "

"Ahem—seat occupied? "

"No. "

The man we have met on a previous occasion, Professor Darlington Ruggles, settled himself beside the late comer.

"Ahem—fine evening. "

A grunt answered the Professor's attempt to be sociable. At length, after casting a keen glance about the car, to find that but few passengers were present, and those of but little consequence, Professor Ruggles said:

"He's in the next car. "

"Yes. I'd like to get my clutches onto him agin. "

"You had him once? "

"Yes, but he had help, and escaped. Do you imagine he's on the trail? "

"Certainly, " answered Professor Ruggles.

"Then he'll get off to-night. "

"I hope so; but you must be cautious. "

"Trust me for that. "

"Have you formulated a plan? "

"None. "

"Then let me help you. "

"I'll be glad to do so. "

"If we can get the fellow onto the platform the work will be easy. You understand, Sam? "

"I reckon. "

"Once he goes over nothing can save him. "

"True, but how will we git the cuss outside? "

"Easy's preaching. I'll go and introduce myself and get him to wait this car to try an excellent brand of cigars—see? " And the Professor chuckled audibly,

"I expect it's easier said than done, " returned the thickset villain. "Twixt you 'n me, Ruggles, Dyke Darrel's cut his eye teeth, an' he don't walk into no traps with his eyes open, I can tell you that. "

"Well, we'll see about it. I flatter myself that I'm sharper than any detective that ever lived. "

Then, adjusting his glasses, the sunset-haired Professor left his seat and walked down the aisle to the door. He came hurrying back with an interested, perhaps anxious look on his countenance.

"Now's your time, Sam, " whispered Professor Ruggles; "the fellow's on the platform smoking! "

This was fully two hours after the thickset man first stepped upon the train. He at once came to his feet, and sauntered in a careless manner to the door. The night was not dark, and the man could plainly see a dark form leaning against the end of the opposite car, a bright red gleam showing the end of his cigar.

It was indeed Dyke Darrel, who had come out upon the platform to cool his heated brow and reflect on the situation, while he smoked a cigar for its soothing influence.

He could not drive the thought of Harry Bernard and the train robbery from his mind. He remembered that the young man had left Woodburg suddenly the fall before, and nothing had been seen or heard from him by his friends since, until Dyke's meeting him so strangely in St. Louis. It was barely possible that the assault and the rescue by young Bernard were part of a deep-laid plot. Dyke Darrel possessed a suspicious mind, and he could not reconcile appearances with the innocence of young Harry Bernard.

Deeply meditating, the detective scarcely noticed the opening of the car door opposite his position. His gaze, however, soon met the form of a man as he stepped across the narrow opening between the coaches.

The detective was instantly on the alert. He was not to be caught napping, as he had been once before that night.

The moment the stranger passed to his platform, Dyke Darrel faced him with a drawn revolver in his hand.

"Mr., I want a word with you. "

Thus uttered the thick-set passenger, and then Dyke Darrel recognized the man who had boarded the train at the first station outside of St. Louis.

"What is it you want? " demanded the detective shortly.

"THIS! "

With the word, the man lunged forward. Divining his movement, Dyke Darrel sank suddenly to the steps, and his assailant plunged headlong from the train!

CHAPTER IX.

WORDS THAT STARTLE.

It seemed a terrible plunge into eternity. Not for one moment did the detective lose his presence of mind, however. Straightening, he reached up and grasped the bell-cord.

Ere many seconds the train came to a stop.

"Man on the track, " said Dyke Darrel when the conductor came hurrying to see what was the trouble.

Lanterns were at once brought into requisition, and men went back to look for the body of the detective's assailant.

No one imagined that he could possibly plunge from the speeding train and escape death. Dyke Darrel moved along confidently expecting to look upon the bruised corpse of the outlaw who had attempted his destruction.

He met with disappointment.

No man was found.

"He must have been a tough one to have jumped the train without receiving a scratch, " said a voice in the ear of the detective, as he flashed the rays of a lantern down on the track.

Dyke Darrel glanced at the speaker, a gentleman with enormous red beard, and rather worn silk hat.

This was the detective's first introduction to Professor Ruggles.

"I've no doubt of his being tough, " answered Dyke Darrel.

"How did it happen? "

"I think the fellow intended to throw me off the train. "

"Goodness! is that so? What was the trouble about? "

"No trouble that I am aware of. I did not know the man. "

"Then it's likely he mistook you for some one else. "

Dyke Darrel eyed the speaker keenly. There seemed to be nothing suspicious about the Professor, however, and soon after the detective dismissed him from his mind.

"All aboard! " shouted the conductor, a little later, and soon the train was speeding northward at a rapid rate.

Dyke Darrel went into the rear car, and sat down to meditate on his adventure. He realized that his death had been planned by enemies to law and order, and he believed by the ones who were anxious to throw him off the trail of the outlaws who perpetrated the crime on the midnight express a few nights before.

It did not seem possible that the man who had attempted to throw him from the train, and had gone over himself, had escaped unharmed.

Doubtless, though badly hurt, he had managed to drag himself away from the immediate vicinity of the track, where he had remained secreted until the brief search was over.

Since his fall was unexpected, it was not likely that any of the villain's friends were in the vicinity, and so it might be an easy matter to trace the outlaw. Dyke Darrel formed a plan of operation at once, and rose to leave the train at the next stop.

"Do you get off here? "

Dyke Darrel was somewhat surprised to see Harper Elliston on the platform of the little station.

"I stop here, " said Dyke. "And you? "

"I thought of going to Chicago. "

"Postpone your trip then. I wish to consult with you on a matter of importance. "

The tall gentleman hesitated.

The train began to move.

"You must decide quickly, " cried the detective.

Elliston walked the length of the narrow platform, with his hand on the car rail, his satchel in the other hand. His hand fell from the rail, and the express swept swiftly away in the darkness.

"Anything to accommodate, Dyke. I had some business of importance to transact in Chicago, but it can wait. "

"I am sorry if I put you to extra expense, Harper, but I wish to consult with one whom I can trust. I've got a devilish mean work on hand, " said Dyke Darrel in an explanatory tone.

"You know I am always ready to assist you, Dyke. Is it a criminal case? "

"Yes; the last on record. "

"The express crime? "

"Yes. "

"I mistrusted as much. You have been down the road? "

"To St. Louis! "

"Exactly. "

"I took a young offender down who escaped from prison last winter. I think the officers will look after him more closely in the future. "

"Who was it? "

"Martin Skidway. "

"I don't call to mind the name, now. "

Lights in the distance showed that the village contained one public-house at least. So there the two men repaired.

Mr. Elliston quaffed a glass of wine, while the detective would take nothing but a cigar. Repairing to a room, the two men sat and conversed for some time in the most confidential way.

Dyke Darrel gave his friend an account of his adventure on the train, which had induced him to stop off and investigate.

The reader may imagine that it was extremely indiscreet for the detective to give away his plans to Elliston, but Dyke Darrel had known this man for more than a year, had visited him in New York, and found him to be well thought of there, and he had more than once confided in him, to find him as true as steel.

At this time the detective believed Elliston to be the best friend he had in the world. He knew the New Yorker to be a man of great ability and thoroughly acquainted with the world, and more than once he had done a good turn for Darrel. Why then should he not trust him? In fact, Dyke Darrel had noticed the growing interest Mr. Elliston took in his sister, and it pleased him. Looking upon him as almost a brother, it is little wonder that Dyke Darrel took the man from Gotham into his confidence to a considerable extent.

"I think you did the right thing in leaving the train to look after this villain, " said Elliston, when he had heard the detective's story; "but you must be aware that you run a great risk in going about the country without disguise, avowedly in search of the perpetrators of the express robbery. Of course, this man has friends, and they will not hesitate to shoot or stab, as they did in the case of the express messenger. "

"Certainly—"

"But, my dear Dyke, had I not happened at the station you might have run into a trap. I have reason to believe there are many lawless characters in this neighborhood. It strikes me that the man knew what he was about when he assaulted you at this point on the road. "

To this, however, Dyke Darrel did not agree. He believed that the villain who attempted his murder sought the first favorable opportunity for his fell work, regardless of time and place.

Early the next morning the detective and his friend hired a horse and buggy of the hotel proprietor, and set off down the road to the scene of the "accident. "

Dyke Darrel was confident that he could find the spot, and, sure enough, he was not far out in his reckoning. When in the vicinity of where he believed the man had left the train, Darrel's quick eye caught sight of a group of men standing under a shed, on the further side of a distant field.

"There is some cause of excitement over yonder, " remarked Dyke Darrel, as he drew rein, and pointed with his whip.

"It seems to mean something, " admitted Elliston.

"I propose to investigate. "

Securing his horse, Dyke Darrel vaulted the fence, and, closely followed by Elliston, made his way across the field.

A dozen men and boys stood about, regarding some object with commiserating glances.

Dyke Darrel pushed his way into the crowd, and was not disappointed in what he saw—a man lying prostrate on some blankets, with white face and blood-stained garments.

"We found him jest off the railroad, in a fence-corner, " said one of the countrymen. "He'll never git up an' walk agin. "

"Has he said anything? "

This last question was put by Harper Elliston.

"Nary word. He fell off 'n ther train last night, I reckon. "

Elliston knelt and felt the man's pulse.

"He lives, " said the New Yorker, "but there isn't much life; he cannot last long. "

"A little brandy might revive him, " said Dyke Darrel. "I would like to have him speak; it is of the utmost importance. "

"Indeed it is, " cried Elliston. "Where is the flask of brandy you brought from the train, Dyke? "

"In the buggy. "

"Send a man for it. "

"I will go myself; " and Dyke Darrel set off at a rapid walk across the field. At the same moment the man on the blanket groaned and opened his eyes.

"How do you feel, my man? " questioned Elliston.

"I—I'm used up. "

"It looks so. "

Elliston bent lower.

"You're going to die, Sam, sure's shooting, " he said in a whisper at the ear of the prostrate wretch.

A groan was the only reply.

"Do you hear me, Sam? "

"Yes, I—I hear, " was the faint answer.

Placing his lips to the ear of the man, Elliston continued to whisper for some seconds.

Soon the detective returned with a flask of brandy, which he at once placed to the lips of the bruised and helpless wreck. A few sips seemed to revive the man wonderfully.

"Tell me your name, my man, " questioned the detective, eagerly.

"Sam Swart. "

"Do you realize your condition? You have but a few hours to live, and if you wish to free your mind, we will listen. "

Elliston stood at the man's feet, facing him with folded arms, while the kneeling detective addressed himself to the apparently dying man.

"I haven't nothing to tell. "

"See here, Mr. Swart, it is better that you tell what you know. Do justice for once, and it may be better with you in the hereafter. You attempted to murder me last night, and I believe you had a hand in the death of Arnold Nicholson and the robbery of the express. "

"I—I did, but he coaxed me into it, " articulated the poor wretch in a husky voice. Elliston caught the words, and his cheek suddenly blanched. He was outwardly calm, however.

Dyke Darrel bent low to catch the faint words of Swart. It was evident that the man was rapidly sinking, and the detective was terribly anxious to get at the truth.

"Speak! " he cried, hoarsely, "WHO coaxed you to commit this crime? "

"HE did. The boy and—and Nick was with—with me. "

"But who was the leader—the instigator of the foul deed? "

Close to the swollen lips of the dying man bent the ear of Dyke Darrel, every nerve on the alert to catch the faint reply.

A name was uttered that caused Dyke Darrel to spring to his feet with a great cry.

CHAPTER X.

BLACK HOLLOW.

"What was it? —WHO was it? " cried Harper Elliston, seizing the arm of Dyke Darrel, and penetrating him with a keen glance.

"It does not matter. "

"It does. I have had a suspicion. "

"Well? "

"He uttered the name of Harry Bernard. "

"How could you guess that? "

"Because I have felt it in my bones, " answered the tall New Yorker. "Harry Bernard acted queerly before he left Woodburg the last time, and I have since arrived at the conclusion that he was engaged in some unlawful work. "

"Well, I never entertained such a suspicion, " was all the detective vouchsafed in reply. Then he glanced at the man on the ground.

"See, the fellow is dying. "

It was true. Sam Swart, the miserable outlaw, was swiftly passing away. Half an hour later, when Elliston and the detective returned to their buggy, the would-be murderer of Dyke Darrel lay cold in death under the farmer's shed.

A serious expression pervaded the face of Dyke Darrel, and he scarcely spoke during the drive back to town.

"Did you find your man? " queried the landlord, when our friends returned.

"Yes. "

Elliston entered into an explanation, while Dyke Darrel went up to his room and threw himself into a chair in a thoughtful attitude. His brow became corrugated, and it was evident that the detective was enjoying a spell of the deepest perplexity.

"It must be that the fellow's mind wandered, " mused Dyke Darrel. "Of course I cannot accept as evidence the ragged, half-conscious utterances of a dying man. He spoke of Nick and the boy. There may be something in that. The boy? Who could that be but Martin Skidway? I've suspected him; he is capable of anything in the criminal line. It may be well for me to go to Chicago and visit Martin's Aunt Scarlet. How that woman hates me, simply because I was the means of breaking up a gang of spurious money makers, of whom old Dan Scarlet was the chief. Well, well, the ways of the world are curious enough. By the way, I haven't sent that line to Nell yet. The girl will feel worried if I don't write. "

Then, drawing several postals from his pocket, Dyke Darrel wrote a few lines on one with a pencil, and addressed it to "Miss Nell Darrel, Woodburg. "

Just then Elliston entered.

"When does the next train pass, Harper? "

"In twenty minutes. Will you go on it to Chicago? "

"Not to Chicago. I shall stop half a hundred miles this side, or more. I wish to do a little more investigating. "

"Don't you accept what the dying Swart said as true? "

"Not wholly. "

"Would a dying man be likely to utter a falsehood? "

"I can't say. What is your opinion? "

There was a peculiar look in the eyes of Dyke Darrel, as he put the question.

"I should think there could be no doubt on the subject. "

"Indeed; then you consider that the last name that fell from the lips of Sam Swart was that of the man who instigated the wicked crime on the midnight express? "

"Certainly, that is my opinion. "

Dyke Darrel drew out a cigar and lit it, his friend refusing to take one.

"I can't feel so sanguine as you seem to, Harper. Will you go on? "

"I shall go to Chicago. "

"You do not care to remain with me longer? "

Dyke Darrel regarded his friend closely through a cloud of smoke.

"You forget that I left urgent business to keep you company last night, " answered Mr. Elliston, a tinge of rebuke in his voice.

"I do not. You have my hearty thanks for your disinterested kindness, Harper, " returned Dyke Darrel. "If the delay has cost you anything—-"

"See here, old chum, don't insult me, " cried Elliston, as the detective drew out a well-filled wallet. "I am able and willing to pay my own bills, I hope. "

"Certainly. I meant no offense. "

"It is time we were on the move, Dyke, if we do not wish to miss the up train. "

Dyke Darrel realized the force of his friend's words, and at once made preparations for departure. A little later the two were on board the morning express, speeding Northward. Dyke Darrel informed the conductor of the fate of Sam Swart, the outlaw, but did not intimate that the fellow was a member of the gang of train robbers, whose deed of blood had sent a shudder of horror and indignation throughout the nation.

When the train halted at Black Hollow, the station at which the terrible crime of a few days previous had been discovered, Dyke Darrel arose to go.

"When shall I see you again, Dyke? " questioned Mr. Elliston.

"I am not sure. I shall be in Woodburg next week. "

"I will see you there, then. "

"Very well. "

The detective left the train, and stood alone on the platform of the little station. There were not a dozen houses in sight, and it was not often that the express halted at this place. Here the daring deed of robbers had been discovered. It could not be far from here that the outlaws left the express car, doubtless springing off and escaping in the darkness as the train slowed up to the station.

Not a soul in sight.

Dyke Darrel entered the depot, to see a man standing at the window who had been watching the moving train as it rushed away on its northern course.

"No public house here, sir, " said the man, who proved to be the railway agent, in answer to an inquiry from the detective.

"Then I must find some one who will keep me for a short time, " returned Dyke Darrel. "I am looking for a location in which to open a gun-shop. "

"Guns would sell here, I reckon, " said Mr. Bragg. "I guess maybe I can accommodate you with a stopping-place for a day or two. "

"Thanks. I will pay you well. "

"I'm not a shark, " answered the agent. "You see that brown house up yonder, in the edge of that grove? "

"Yes. "

"That's my place. I can't go up just now; but you may tell my wife that I sent you, and it will be all right. "

Dyke Darrel sauntered down past several dingy-looking dwellings until he came to the house of Mr. Bragg. It was really the most respectable dwelling in the place, which could not have been famous for its fine residences.

The aspect about was not calculated to prepossess one in favor of the country. Somehow, it seemed to the detective that Black Hollow was half a century behind the age. Mrs. Bragg was a shy, ungainly female, and not at all communicative.

Darrel occupied the remainder of the day in exploring the country in the vicinity. A creek crossed the railroad and entered a deep gulch, the sides of which were lined with a dense growth of bushes.

An ill-defined path led down the steep side of the gulch, and was lost to sight in the dense growth at the bottom.

Dyke Darrel followed this path, and soon found himself in a dense wood that seemed to cover a strip of bottom land. Moving on, the deep shadows soon encompassed him on every side.

A solemn stillness seemed to pervade the place, and a feeling of loneliness came over the detective.

"What a splendid place for secreting plunder, or hiding from officers of the law. "

It was almost dark ere the detective turned to retrace his steps. The narrow path grew indistinct, and it was only with the utmost difficulty that Dyke Darrel kept his course.

The snapping of a dry twig suddenly startled him.

This sound was followed almost instantly by the whip-like crack of a rifle. A stinging sensation on the cheek, together with the whistle of a deadly bullet, warned Dyke Darrel of a narrow escape.

CHAPTER XI.

POOR SIBYL!

Instantly the detective drew his revolver and sought shelter behind a tree. Then he gazed sharply in the direction from whence the sound of the rifle had come.

A faint line of smoke in the distance alone met the gaze of Dyke Darrel.

It was evident that some one had fired upon him with murderous intent. This was the belief of the detective.

"Somebody has dogged my steps; there can be no doubt about that, " answered Dyke Darrel. "I was not wrong in my supposition that Black Hollow is the rendezvous of a gang of outlaws. I wish I had one good man with me to help hunt these scoundrels down. "

The darkness deepened, but no one appeared, and fearing that he would not be able to follow the path if he tarried, Dyke Darrel, with his revolver in hand, ready for use, moved from his shelter, and attempted to make his way out of the labyrinth in which he found himself.

The detective soon lost the path, however, and found himself in a desperate tangle, with the blackness of a dismal night settling down upon the place.

"I'm in a pickle, now, for a fact, " muttered Dyke Darrel. "I was a little indiscreet in coming here so late in the day. It does seem as though I must come out somewhere if I continue to strive. "

Nevertheless, an hour's walk in the dense undergrowth failed to bring the detective to the bank of Black Hollow, or to any opening. "A veritable trap for the unwary, " growled Dyke, as he halted with his back against a tree, with the perspiration oozing from every pore. Even his wiry limbs and muscles were not proof against the tangled nature of the wood into which he had so coolly entered.

Dyke Darrel was not in a pleasant mood as he stood meditating on the situation.

"It looks now as though I was destined to remain in the wood all night. "

It was not a pleasing prospect.

The detective was on the point of making one more effort to break through the tangle that encompassed him, when something caught his eye that sent a thrill to his heart.

It was the glimmer of a light.

It did not seem to be far away, and Dyke Darrel resumed his fight with the thickets with renewed courage. In a little time he entered a glade in the woods, to find himself standing in near proximity to a low log cabin, through a narrow window of which a light glimmered.

"Some one lives here, it seems. "

Dyke Darrel moved forward cautiously, for he still believed that the wood was the haunt of outlaws, and this very house might be the den where the plunder of many raids was secreted.

Soon the detective stood on a little rise of ground, in such a position that he could peer into the window. The interior of a small, poorly-furnished apartment met his gaze. Beside the glowing embers of a wood fire in a box stove crouched a human figure, seemingly the only occupant of the lone log cabin.

There was a wealth of golden hair flashing in the firelight, and the black robe covered the form of what seemed to be a beautiful woman.

As may be supposed, the detective was surprised at the sight. After a moment of reflection he resolved to enter the cabin.

Striding to the door, he rapped gently. No answer came, and the detective rapped again. This time the door was cautiously opened, and a white face peered out.

"Who's there? "

"A traveler who has lost his way. "

"You cannot come in. Sibyl isn't afraid, but she wishes to be alone. "

Nevertheless, the woman stood aside and held the door wide. This seemed invitation enough, and the detective at once crossed the floor, and pushed to the door at his back

The female receded before him, and stood at the far side of the room, with both hands extended, waving them gently up and down.

"Come no nearer, sir; Sibyl would view you from afar. There, stand where you are, and do not move. It may be that you are the one I have been looking for all these years. "

The speaker was evidently young, and possessed a weirdly beautiful face, that strangely attracted Dyke Darrel. He stood still and watched her singular movements curiously.

She drew a morocco case from her bosom, opened it, and gazed at something, evidently a picture, long and earnestly. She seemed to be comparing the face of the picture with that of her visitor.

Dyke Darrel was puzzled, and somewhat pleased.

"No, you are not my Hubert; he was a nobler looking gentleman by far. "

"Will you permit me to look at the picture, Miss—"

"No, no; I dare not trust it out of my hands. I promised him, you know, and I must not disappoint Hubert, for he is very exacting. Hark! "

The girl secreted her prize, and lifted a warning hand.

"Don't you hear his step? It is Hubert—dear, dear Hubert—come back to comfort his poor Sybil after these long, weary years. "

A low, startling laugh fell from her lips at the last. She darted across the floor, and flung the door wide, peering out into the darkness.

A solemn, awful silence followed, then the door was sharply closed, and the queerly acting girl faced Dyke Darrel once more. She looked weirdly beautiful, with a mass of golden hair falling below her taper waist, her face white as the winter's snow, almost too white for the living.

So she stood now; the dancing light from the fire fell full on her countenance, revealing it for the first time plainly to the gaze of the detective.

A low, stunned cry escaped from his lips.

"My God! It is Sibyl Osborne, the Burlington Captain's daughter. "

A low laugh fell from the girl's lips.

She began humming a gay tune, and danced across the room with arms outstretched, as though attempting to fly.

The truth came with stunning force—the poor girl was crazy! Her father, a wealthy Burlington real estate broker, had mysteriously disappeared some months before, and it was supposed that he had met with foul play. Despite the efforts of Dyke Darrel and other detectives, no clew had yet been found of the missing man. The detective had met Sibyl at her father's house, and had regarded her as one both beautiful and accomplished. To meet her as now was a terrible revelation indeed.

No wonder Dyke Darrel was stunned.

For some moments he stood in pained silence, watching the antics of the poor unfortunate.

"Hubert will come, Hubert will come, " she sung, as she glided back and forth across the floor.

What had caused this awful calamity? Dyke Darrel asked this question in saddened thoughtfulness, as he gazed upon the beautiful wreck before him.

"Tell me that Hubert will come, sir, and then I won't believe that he wrote that cruel letter, " cried Sibyl, in a mournful voice, pausing in front of the detective. "I cannot tell you unless you show me the letter, " returned Dyke Darrel, resolving to humor her.

Quickly she drew from her bosom a letter and placed it in the detective's hand.

He drew it from the wrapper, hoping to learn something that might give him a clew to the situation.

This is what he read:

"MISS SIBYL OSBORNE: I am sorry to inform you that I cannot see you again. I am off for Europe on my wedding tour. Forget me as soon as possible.

"H. VANDER. "

"Do you think my Hubert could write anything so cruel? " she questioned, as he handed the missive back to her.

"It doesn't seem possible, " answered Dyke Darrel.

It was evident to his mind that the girl had become crazed on account of her father's disappearance and the treachery of her lover. The detective's heart beat sympathetically for the poor wronged girl. It was his duty to see the girl safely on her way to the Burlington ere he continued his search for the assassins of Arnold Nicholson. One had already given up his account, but there were others yet to punish.

While Dyke Darrel stood debating what course to pursue, under the remarkable change in circumstances, the mad girl uttered a sudden, sharp cry.

"See! it is Hubert, my Hubert! come at last! "

A look of mad joy sped across the white face, as one slender arm was extended, pointing toward the window. Dyke Barrel followed with his eyes, and then he, too, uttered an involuntary cry.

Glued to the narrow pane was a face that was startling in the intensity of its ghastly pallor, but it was not this that sent an involuntary exclamation to the lips of the railroad detective.

The face at the window was that of his friend, HARPER ELLISTON! His presence here was one of the mysteries of that eventful night.

CHAPTER XII.

A BURNING TRAP.

For some moments Dyke Darrel stared at the face in the window without moving. How came Harper Elliston in the woods at Black Hollow, when he ought to have been in Chicago, according to his expressed intentions of the previous day?

With a sudden, wild scream the crazed Sibyl darted across the floor, and thrust her hands against the window with such violence as to burst the glass, cutting her hands severely in the operation.

"Hubert! Hubert! come at last! " The girl staggered back and sank in a paroxysm to the floor.

It was indeed a startling affair, yet Dyke Darrel did not lose his presence of mind. He hurried to the door and opened it, springing outside quickly.

"Elliston, I want you. "

Dyke Darrel stood by the broken window now, but the man he had expected to find was not there. The apparition had vanished as though fleeing into the upper air.

Again the detective called the name of his friend, but without receiving a reply.

Here was a mystery indeed.

Had that face at the window been an optical delusion, after all?

Dyke Darrel was not superstitious, yet in the present case a queer feeling oppressed him, and an awful misgiving entered his mind.

"I cannot believe that the face at the window was other than that of Elliston's; and yet she called him Hubert. It must be that there is a mistake somewhere, and it seems to me that the mad girl is more apt to be deceived than I. "

Once more Dyke Darrel returned to the house.

Sibyl Osborne lay in a dead faint on the floor. The detective began chafing her hands at once, and loosened her corsage.

A morocco case fell to the floor.

It was the one containing the alleged picture of Hubert Vander. Under the circumstances Dyke Darrel believed he was justified in examining it.

He opened the case, and was soon gazing at the face of a handsome man.

Although smoothly shaved, the face of the photograph was that of Harper Elliston!

A horrid suspicion now took possession of the detective's brain.

Securing case and photograph on his own person, Dyke Darrel proceeded in his efforts to bring the girl back to life.

He was soon rewarded.

"It was Hubert. "

These were the first words uttered by the girl when she opened her eyes. Her hands were stained with blood from cuts made by the glass.

She gazed at the blood, and grew suddenly deathly pale.

"My God! he has tried to murder me! "

Then she came to her feet, flinging her tangled golden hair about wildly, and shrank to the far corner of the room.

"You have nothing to fear from me, Miss Osborne, " said Dyke. "I am your friend. "

"And Hubert's friend? "

"Yes, Hubert's friend, too. "

"Who did this, then? "

She held up her bleeding hands.

He tried to explain, and she seemed to understand partially, so much so as to lose her fear of the detective.

She began to laugh soon, and the late adventure seemed to pass entirely from her mind. Dyke was glad to have it so.

"Will you not lie down and rest? " he said presently. "We have a long journey to go in the morning. "

"Where? To Hubert? "

"Yes, to Hubert. "

Her great blue eyes regarded him wistfully, and a throb of pain entered his heart at thought of the beautiful girl's misfortune. There was growing in his heart a dangerous feeling, one that boded no good to Harper Elliston, should that man prove to be as he now believed, the Hubert Vander of the mad girl's dreams.

"Take me to Hubert now, kind sir. I know you can do so, and I shall die if he does not keep his word with me. He will never betray a poor girl—such a gentleman, and so good? Yes, I will do anything to please you, for it will bring dear Hubert back. "

She went up and laid both hands on the shoulders of the detective, and looked so mournfully into his face as to touch the tenderness in his nature deeply. His heart bled for the girl who had been the victim of a villain's wiles.

"Sit down and rest, Miss Osborne; we will try and find Hubert in the morning. "

"You are very kind. "

She seemed gentle and subdued now. It was the calm after the storm. Dyke saw that he was not recognized, however, and the madness was not gone from the poor girl's brain.

It was a very sad case, indeed.

Several stools were in the room, and some blankets hung against the further wall, proving that some one had lately occupied the cabin. Undoubtedly it had been used as a hiding-place for outlaws, and it was a question in the mind of the detective as to how soon the cabin would be revisited. The presence of the insane girl necessarily altered his plans somewhat. He could not leave her to perish in the woods.

Removing the blankets from the wall, Dyke Darrel improvised a bed for the poor girl, and induced her to lie thereon. He then replenished the fire with some dry sticks that lay beside the stove, since the night air was chill, and sat himself upon the floor, with his head reclining against the logs. Before doing this, however, he had taken the precaution to secure the only door with a wooden latch that had been made for the purpose.

The window, of course, he was unable to secure.

It did not seem hardly safe to sleep under the circumstances, but Dyke Darrel was very tired, having been without much rest for several nights, and he was on the present occasion extremely drowsy.

Resolving not to fall into a deep slumber, the detective sat with his revolver at his side, and went off into the land of dreams before he was aware of it.

Dyke Darrel slept heavily.

A crackling sound outside did not reach his ear with sufficient force to waken him. A face peered in at the window, dark and sinister, but the sleeping detective heeded it not.

Another face, girded about with bristling red hair, appeared for a moment, and then receded. Dark forms moved about the cabin without, and engaged in a whispered conversation.

Presently the trees and bushes became visible, and there was a smell of burning wood in the air.

"It is well, " uttered a voice. "They will both perish like rats in a trap. Dyke Darrel, the famous detective, will never be heard of more, and that girl—well, she will be better dead than living. Come, Nick, let us go! "

"You're sure the door's tightly fastened? " "I fixed it so Satan himself could not open it. "

"Good. "

"Let us go! "

"Wait. I'd like to see the curse roast. "

"No, no; that won't do. We'll come in the day time and look at the bones. This old log hut has had its day, and we could not put it to a better use than to make a mausoleum for the man-tracker of the West. "

There was no hesitating after this.

The two men moved swiftly away in the gloom that surrounded the burning cabin.

A choking sensation caused the reclining man in the cabin to stir uneasily.

Presently he opened his eyes.

The room was full of smoke, and red tongues of flame were licking at the logs from every side.

Quickly Dyke Darrel came to his feet. A smell of burning garments filled his nostrils. The bed on which Sibyl Osborne rested was on fire!

"My soul! this is unfortunate, " cried the detective. He was equal to the emergency, however. Springing to the side of the still sleeping girl, Dyke lifted her in his arms and strode to the door.

Quickly he slipped the rude bolt and grasped the latch. It refused to yield.

The door was firmly secured on the outside.

CHAPTER XIII.

A SAD FATE.

For one instant, Dyke Darrel was paralyzed.

It was for a moment only, however. He shook the door furiously, blinded by smoke, and almost strangled by hot air.

The door would not yield.

At this moment, the girl awoke and began to scream. Bits of burning wood fell all about them.

Soon the roof would tumble in with a crash. When that moment came, every living thing must perish within the house.

Dyke Darrel moved to the window, leading Sibyl. She staggered and seemed ready to fall.

"Courage! " he cried, "we will soon be out of this. "

Reaching the narrow window, the detective dashed out sash and glass with a stool, and the air from outside seemed like a breath from fairy land.

"You must go first? "

Dyke Darrel assisted his fair companion to the opening. An instant later she had passed outside.

Then something occurred that quite startled the detective and filled him with intense alarm.

A burning log fell from the side of the cabin with a thud that was sickening. A horrible fear at once took possession of Darrel. With a quick bound he gained the opening, and leaped clear of the burning logs to the ground without.

Turning about he uttered a cry of horror.

Sibyl Osborne lay crushed beneath a black log that was yet smoking with heat. With a herculean effort the detective lifted and flung the log from the poor girl's breast, and then he lifted and carried her beyond the reach of flame and heat, and laid her on a little mound beneath a giant tree.

One glance into the mad girl's face satisfied him of the mournful truth. The falling log had done fatal work, and with his hand clasping hers, Dyke Darrel watched the gasps that grew fainter each moment, until the silence and quietude of eternity rested on all.

"Dead! "

With that one word Dyke Darrel started to his feet and gazed about him. There was a flinty gleam in his keen eyes and a fierce grating of white teeth.

It had been a long time since the railroad detective was moved as at that hour, with the work of human fiends before him.

From the burning cabin his gaze returned to the upturned white face of the dead girl. Pure and lovely as a lily looked the face of the wronged and dead.

"It is better so, perhaps, " muttered the detective.

Had the girl lived she might never have enjoyed an hour of reason. With that dethroned, what could death be but a welcome messenger. And yet the manner of the mad girl's taking off was shocking in the extreme.

Had Dyke Darrel known the way out, he would have taken the corpse in his arms and hurried from the scene at once. As it was, the detective deemed it wise to remain in the vicinity until morning, when it was likely he would have little trouble in making his way out of the woods!

The remaining hours of the night passed slowly. Dyke Darrel dared not sleep, and so he kept his lonely vigil beside the dead, seated in the shadows, with revolver ready to use at a moment's notice.

No interruption came, however, and when the gray streaks of morning dawned the detective breathed easier. He at once went in search of a road that would lead out of the wood.

He met with better success than he had dared hope. He found a path that must have been used by the owner of the cabin, and which it was evident the mad girl had followed in her wanderings.

How long she had been in the cabin the detective had no means of knowing, but it seemed to him evident that she could have been there but a few hours when discovered by him.

The way out of the Black Hollow woods was long and tedious, but Dyke Darrel proved equal to the task, and when he broke cover and entered upon the open ground above, he was glad to see a team approaching, driven by a farmer.

"Hello! What hev' you got there? " cried the man, in open-eyed amazement, when he halted beside the detective and his burden.

"A lady. She was accidentally killed last night. "

"It's awful! "

"I quite agree with you, " returned Dyke Darrel; "but if you will take the woman aboard and drive to the house of Mr. Bragg, I will pay you for it. "

"Of course I will. "

The farmer was garrulous on the way, and it required all the detective's ingenuity to answer his questions promptly, so as not to excite the fellow's suspicions.

The body of the beautiful dead girl was laid in one of Agent Bragg's rooms, and the latter telegraphed to the nearest town of importance for a casket, which arrived at Black Hollow shortly after noon.

"I will attend to shipping it, " said Mr. Bragg. "This is a sad case. It is a wonder to me that somebody did not see the girl yesterday. "

"Possibly she got off at another station. "

"Do you think she came to this vicinity on the cars? "

"Most certainly, " answered the detective.

"Will you go to Chicago now? "

"I am not fully decided, " returned Dyke Darrel. "At what hour does the train pass? "

"Six-fifty to-night. "

"But the down train goes earlier? "

"At four. "

"And at Bloomington I can take the cars for Burlington? " "If you so desire. "

"I will think about it. "

Sauntering along in the afternoon, just in the outskirts of the village, Dyke Darrel came suddenly upon a man standing with his back against a telegraph pole.

"Hello! " ejaculated the detective, as the man turned and faced him.

It was Harper Elliston.

"I thought you were in Chicago, " pursued the mystified Dyke. And then he remembered the face he had seen at the window of the cabin in Black Hollow the previous night. The memory brought a harsh expression to his countenance.

"Ah, you are still here, Dyke. "

Mr. Elliston smiled and held out his hand.

"I don't understand this, " said Dyke Darrel. "You have deceived me in some way, Harper. You were in Black Hollow last night. "

"There you are mistaken, " assured Mr. Elliston; "I stopped off here on the noon train. "

"You did not go to Chicago, then? "

"Yes, I did; but only remained an hour. You see the man I was looking for was not there, but had gone to Burlington, Iowa, and so, remembering that you stopped off here yesterday, I thought I would run down and learn if you had made any discovery. "

"You came at noon? "

"Yes. "

"Why did not you call for me at Bragg's? "

"Are you stopping there? "

"Certainly. If you had inquired for me of the agent here, you would have certainly found me. "

"That's exactly what I did do, and I did not find you; so now, " and Mr. Elliston laughed at the perplexed look on the detective's face.

The actions and words of this man were indeed a puzzle to Dyke Darrel.

"Harper, I want to ask you a plain question——"

"And you want a categorical answer, Mr. Darrel, " interrupted the New Yorker with a laugh.

"I do. "

"Go ahead. "

"Weren't you in Black Hollow last night? "

"Certainly not. I was with a friend at least sixty miles away, near Chicago. "

"Can you prove this? "

"If necessary, of course; but what in the world is the matter, Dyke? I hope you wouldn't accuse me of deception. "

"No. Will you come with me to Bragg's? "

"Certainly. "

And then the two men walked away together. There was a solemn expression pervading the face of Dyke Darrel. He had experienced many strange things during his detective life, but this latest phase puzzled him the most.

He could swear that he saw the face of Elliston at the window of the house in the gulch on the previous night, yet the assertion from his friend that he was fifty miles away at the time seemed honest enough.

Having been long in the detective work, Dyke Darrel had grown to be suspicious, and so he was fast losing faith in the good intentions of his New York friend. He had suddenly resolved on a test that he believed would prove effectual in setting all doubts at rest.

Arrived at the Bragg dwelling, the detective conducted Harper Elliston at once to the room where the remains of the beautiful, dead girl lay encoffined.

CHAPTER XIV

DYKE DARREL ASTOUNDED.

Dyke Darrel lifted a cloth from the face of the dead, and Harper Elliston stood gazing down upon the features of wronged and murdered Sibyl Osborne.

The detective watched the expression of his companion's countenance closely.

With bated breath the man-hunter glued his gaze upon the face of the man bending over the casket.

"What a sad face, and yet most wonderful in its beauty. Who is she? A daughter of the house? "

Harper turned and regarded Dyke Darrel questioningly, a sympathetic look in his black eyes.

"Do you not know her? "

"*I* know her? You forget that I am a stranger in this part of the West, Dyke. "

"She, too, was a stranger here, Elliston. Her home was in Burlington, and she has been brought to this by a villain who ought to pass the remainder of his days behind prison bars, if not conclude them at a rope's end. Do you know Hubert Vander? "

There was a stern ring in the detective's voice, and a look of deep, indignant feeling pervading his face. All the time he kept his gaze riveted on Elliston.

That gentleman stood the ordeal without flinching, however.

"Hubert Vander? The name is a new one to me, Dyke. "

"Indeed! "

A sneer curled the lip of the detective.

"What do you mean by that? " questioned Mr. Elliston. "Am I to understand that you connect ME in any way with this girl's death, or that I am a friend to this Hubert Vander of whom you speak? "

"Your pretended indignation will not deceive, Harper Elliston. Look at THIS, and tell me what you think of it, " said Dyke Darrel, with the sternness of steel.

The detective laid the photograph he had obtained in the Black Hollow cabin in the hand of Mr. Elliston.

The New Yorker did start then.

He gazed long and constantly at the pictured face.

"What have you to say now, Harper Elliston? " demanded Dyke Darrel, in an awful voice.

"It is a mighty close resemblance, " returned the gentleman. "Where did you obtain this, Dyke? "

"From Sibyl Osborne. "

"Sibyl Osborne? "

"She who lies before you. If that is not YOUR portrait, and if you are not the man who murdered Captain Osborne and ruined his daughter, then I am out of my senses. "

With the words Dyke Darrel presented a cocked revolver at the heart of the cool, smiling villain before him.

The smile left the New Yorker's face, and a serious expression followed it.

"What? You draw a pistol on me, Dyke Darrel? I am surprised, " cried Mr. Elliston in an injured tone. "I did not imagine that you could lose confidence in me, let what would happen. Can it be that our friendship was but a brittle cord, after all? "

"I cannot remain friendly when my confidence has been betrayed. "

"And you deem me a most hardened scoundrel? Of course you will give me a hearing. You are an upholder of law, and do not approve of lynching. Here, put on the handcuffs, Dyke, and take me to prison. You will be sorry for this some time, but now that circumstances are against me your friendship falls to the ground. I did not expect such treatment. However, I can live through it; but I shall never feel toward you as I have in times past. Put on the irons, Dyke. Why do you hesitate? "

"There is a chance for a mistake, of course, " said the detective,

"I am glad you admit that much. "

"Is that your photograph? "

"You said it belonged to a young lady! "

"But is it a photograph of your face? "

"It is not. "

"You swear it? "

"I do. "

"And you were not in Black Hollow, last night? "

"I was not. "

"Swear it?

"I swear it. "

"You did not know this dead girl? "

Dyke Darrel pointed toward the face in the coffin.

"I did not. "

"Will you swear to this also? "

"With my hand on my heart I swear. "

The white hand of Mr. Elliston was laid impressively against his bosom.

There was such a look of honest earnestness on the man's face it was impossible to doubt, and Dyke Darrel was forced to forego arresting the New Yorker then and there.

If he was not fully satisfied, he did not permit Elliston to note the fact.

"I did but try you, Harper, " Dyke Darrel said with a smile, extending his hand. "You are true as steel and I am glad to find it so. I have endured misery since last night, because I feared, and came to believe otherwise. "

"You will trust me as of old? "

"Yes. "

"Thanks. Now tell me all about the facts regarding this poor girl. "

Dyke Darrel did as requested, although he kept back some things that he did not deem it necessary for Mr. Elliston to know.

"And you saw this Hubert Vander peering into the cabin window — the man who looks like me! "

"I did. "

"Well, it's pretty tough, and no mistake, to have a fellow of such villainous character circulating about in this region. I hope I won't be hung for his crime by indignant citizens. I agree with you that this Hubert Vander is a sleek villain, and that hanging is too good for him. It does seem that you made an important discovery last night, however. "

"Explain. "

"This man Vander no doubt murdered Captain Osborne. "

"I am led to think so myself, " said Dyke Darrel.

"He also jilted the Captain's daughter, if no worse, and the two sorrows turned the poor girl's brain. It is a sad and terrible case. I feel deeply interested, and hope to see the scoundrel who looks like me brought to justice. "

"I am glad to hear you say so. "

"Furthermore I have another idea. "

"Proceed. "

"It is undoubtedly this Vander who planned the robbery of the midnight express. A man who could deceive one so beautiful as this girl, would not hesitate to do anything to feather his own nest. "

"Again I agree with you. "

"Evidently it was either this man, or friends of his, who fastened the door of the cabin, and fired it with the hope of destroying the detective who was dogging them so closely. "

"True, I had thought of that. "

"And here's another thing. "

"Well? "

"May not this Vander and his friends conclude that the man-hunter perished in the flames, if they fail to see him again? A disguise would fix that easily, you know. "

"No, that will not go down. "

"Why not? "

"My enemies will visit the ruins of the cabin, and failing to discover skeletons, will learn the truth. "

"That does not necessarily follow. "

"I think it does. I may act on your suggestion, however, " returned Dyke Darrel.

"And put on a disguise? "

"Yes. "

"What will it be? "

The detective laughed.

"Don't ask me, Harper, " he said. "Of what use a disguise that my friends all understood? "

"Is this because you fear to trust me, after what has happened, Dyke?"

"No; but I prefer to keep my own counsel! "

"And you are right. "

"I am glad you admit it. "

The friends then left the room.

At the last moment, Dyke Darrel decided on accompanying the remains of Captain Osborne's daughter to Burlington. He realized that it was the proper thing to do. Elliston parted with the detective, telling him that he meant to return to Woodburg for the present, and would meet him there on his return from the Iowa city.

It was a sad duty that led the railroad detective to revisit Burlington, which he had last looked upon in the fall, shortly after Captain Osborne's disappearance.

Arrived in the bustling Western city, Dyke Darrel was met at the depot by a surprise. An officer laid his hand on the detective's shoulder, and said:

"You are my prisoner, young man. "

"Eh? Well, now, what is this for? " demanded Dyke Darrel angrily.

"FOR THE MURDER OF CAPTAIN OSBORNE AND HIS DAUGHTER! "

Dyke Darrel felt the cold muzzle of a revolver touch his temple at the last.

CHAPTER XV.

A BAFFLED VILLAIN.

In the meantime Harper Elliston, true to his word for once at least, left the train at the Woodburg depot on the same morning that his young detective friend arrived in Burlington.

Repairing to his room at the hotel, the New Yorker remained until the dinner hour. After this he turned his steps in the direction of the Darrel Cottage.

"I suppose Nell Darrel will be delighted to see me, " chuckled Elliston, as he walked up the steps and rang the bell.

Aunt Jule opened the door. "Marse Dyke ain't home. "

"But Miss Nell is, I suppose. "

"Yes, and deed, sir; she's got company, and can't see no one fur de present, " cried the grinning negress, quickly.

"Company? A lot of chattering girls, I suppose? "

"No; a young gemmen — —"

"A gentleman? "

The frown that blackened the brows of Harper Elliston was not pleasant to see. He was not pleased that Nell should receive other male company than himself.

"I will enter. I think she will see me when she knows who has come, " said he, pushing past the negress, and entering the front room.

He seated himself in an armchair, and proceeded to coolly await the coming of the mistress of the house.

Soon Nell Darrel came in. Her face was suffused with smiles, which evidenced that she had heard good news. Elliston, however, flattered himself that it was his coming that caused the pleased look on the face of the detective's sister.

"A pleasant day, Mr. Elliston. "

"Rather. "

He rose and held out his hand. She did not accept it, much to his chagrin.

"Aren't you glad to see me, Nell? " he queried. "I've been absent almost a week, and I thought you would be longing for my company by this time. "

A smile of self-assurance crossed his dark face.

"I have no reason to regard you with any more consideration than on your former visit, " she said. "Have you seen my brother? "

"Yes. "

"Where is he now? "

"In Iowa, I presume. "

"He is well? "

"He was when I parted with him, a short time since. You haven't heard from him? "

"Yes. He was then in a small town in the South or West, I believe. "

Thus they chatted for some time.

During the past few days a desperate resolve had taken possession of Elliston's brain. He admired the pretty Nell now more than ever, and he was determined to make one more effort to win her regard before going to extremes.

That morning he had braced his nerves with several draughts of brandy, and the fumes yet affected him, thus rendering him extremely imprudent, to say the least.

"Nell, Jule tells me you had company when I came. Who was it? "

"A gentleman. "

"Aye, but his name? "

The man's eyes glittered, and seemed to pierce with their keenness to the soul of the girl who sat in front of him. She could smell his breath, too, and the fact that he had been drinking made her a little nervous.

She was anxious for him to depart.

"He is not one of your acquaintances, " replied Nell, evasively.

"But one of yours, it seems, " sneered the man, in a tone that was the least bit disrespectful.

"Mr. Elliston, did you come here to insult me? "

"Certainly not, " he answered in a gentler tone. "Forgive me, Nellie; I can't abide having another win the affections of one I so much covet. If you only knew, Nell — —"

"Mr. Elliston, don't. "

Both came to their feet.

He advanced and seized her hands once more; nay, he suddenly flung one arm about her slender waist and drew her closely, at the same time imprinting a kiss on her cheek.

"I love you, Nell, and will not give you up. Fly with me, darling, where no odious friends may come between us! "

"Villain, release me! "

Nell struggled with desperate energy, but she was as a child in the hands of the tall scoundrel.

"No, no, little girl, I will not permit you to escape. I mean to make it impossible for you to wed another, " grated the man, in a meaning voice, that sent a shudder of horror to the heart of pure Nell Darrel.

Lucky was it for the girl that her visitor had not yet left the house.

Nell screamed aloud, and then the hand of Elliston was pressed over her pretty mouth. Had the man been in his sober senses, he would never have attempted such bold work; but when in liquor Harper Elliston was far from prudent.

"No nonsense now, " he sneered.

And then a door opened; a slender form crossed the floor, and as Elliston turned to confront the new-comer he received a straight left-hander in the chest that sent him back reeling.

Gasping, and very red, Nell started aside, and held out her hand with a low cry of alarm.

The stalwart Elliston soon regained his equilibrium, and faced the one who had dealt him such a furious blow—a slender youth not yet out of his teens, yet in whose blue eyes flashed a determined spirit.

"Scoundrel! " ejaculated Elliston.

He stood glaring at the boy with the venom of a mad serpent in his black eyes.

"Get from this house, or I will call the police and have you put in the cooler, " said the boy, quickly, standing with clenched hands in front of Nell, and returning the tall man's scowls with interest.

"I'll smash every bone in your body, you insignificant little snipe, " roared Elliston. Instead, however, of making the attempt, the man drew a small derringer from his pocket, and lifting the hammer, leveled it at the head of his youthful assaulter.

"Gentlemen, please, please desist, " pleaded Nell in a shaky voice. "This is no place for a quarrel. "

"It isn't, I admit, " returned the boy, "but this sneak brought it about, and now the odds are so much against him, he has recourse to a deadly weapon. There is just that difference between us, Harper Elliston. "

The New Yorker started as the youth pronounced his name. He imagined that he was not known to the boy.

"You see, I know you, " proceeded the boy, noticing the man start. "I have had the villain Elliston pretty well described to me, and know that your act just now justifies me in calling you by that name. Shoot, coward, if you dare. "

There was a cool defiance in the blue eyes of the boy, that won the admiration of Elliston in spite of his anger.

"No, the game is too small, " retorted Elliston, lowering his weapon. "I cannot afford to tarnish an honorable reputation by shedding the blood of a child. I shall, nevertheless, remember you, young man, and on the proper occasion give you the thrashing you so richly deserve. "

A look from Nell Darrel cut short the words that trembled on the lips of the youth.

"I bid you good afternoon, Miss Darrel, " and Elliston bowed and walked to the door. "I will see you again and explain matters. "

The door opened and closed, and the smooth villain was gone.

"Thank Heaven! " murmured Nell. "It might have been worse, " said the boy. "I did not miss my guess when I called him Elliston? "

"No. "

"I thought not. You can see now that Harry Bernard had good reason for warning you to beware of Harper Elliston! "

"I can see it plainly enough, " returned the girl. "When will Harry come to Woodburg? "

"I understand how anxious you are, " said the boy, with a smile. "Harry is assisting Dyke to ferret out the railroad express crime, and it may be some weeks before he comes to this part of the State. I think he will be satisfied to know that you are true to him. It was his knowledge of Elliston's villainy that induced him to send me to see you with a note of warning. "

"I am thankful for his kindness, Mr. Ender. "

"Everybody calls me Paul, Miss Darrel. "

"And everybody (that is my friends), all call me Nell, " returned the girl, with a pleasant little laugh.

"Let it be Nell and Paul then, " and the boy joined in her laugh, thus aiding in banishing the shadows of the day. Harry Bernard's youthful messenger soon after departed, promising to call again on the following day, when he might have another message from young Bernard, who was still supposed to be in St. Louis.

In the meantime the angry and discomfited Elliston repaired to the hotel and made hasty preparations for departure.

He left on the first train for Chicago.

It was late in the evening that Mrs. Scarlet, in her den on Clark street, was roused from a nap she was indulging in, with her head against the wall, by a sharp rap at the door.

Rousing up, she went to see who had come.

She admitted a man with a plug hat and red whiskers.

Professor Darlington Ruggles.

"Aren't you glad to see me, Madam? "

He held out a white set of digits.

"No—why should I be glad? "

She accepted the proffer of friendship, however, and shoved a rickety old chair for her visitor's use.

"I'll tell you why. Because I am the best friend you've got in Chicago."

"That wouldn't be saying much, " and Mrs. Scarlet laughed harshly.

"Wouldn't it? "

"Didn't I say so? Nobody comes to see me now since poor Nephew Martin was taken from me. I feel about ready to die but for one thing. "

"And that? "

"REVENGE! "

Her eyes snapped in their hollow sockets and the withered bosom heaved with inward emotion.

Mr. Ruggles emitted a laugh.

He was evidently pleased at the condition of the woman's feelings.

"I am glad to find you in this condition, Madam, " he said, after a brief pause. "I am here to tell you how you can be revenged, if I mistake not the object on whom your hatred rests.

"It's that infernal Dyke Darrel. "

"I knew it. You would smile and feel happy to see him suffer? "

"It would be as beefsteak to a starving man, " said the woman, savagely.

"Then listen. He has a most charming sister living in one of the interior towns of the State. She is the only relative he has in the wide world. You can strike the railroad detective through Nell Darrel. "

"Yes, yes—go on. "

"He is away most of his time, as you doubtless know ——"

"And the girl is alone? "

"Save for an old negress. Don't interrupt me, please, until I tell you the exact situation. One of my acquaintances, a gentleman of means, and a mean gentleman, for that matter, wishes to get this girl into his possession. What object he may have does not matter, so long as he is willing to pay big for the work. All that is required of you, Mrs. Scarlet, is to furnish a room, and see that when once inside, Miss Darrel does not escape nor communicate with the outside world. Do you understand? "

"I do. "

"And you will consent to act as this girl's keeper for a time? "

"Yes, yes, " cried the woman, with eager emphasis, and then a low, half-suppressed sneeze startled them both.

Professor Darlington Ruggles sprang up and looked toward the door. It stood ajar, and through the opening peered a masked face, centered with a pair of glittering eyes.

Uttering a mad cry, Ruggles drew a concealed revolver and, leveling at the head, fired.

CHAPTER XVI.

NELL MISSING.

The reader can imagine the indignation of the railroad detective when he found himself arrested by the Burlington officer.

"I beg your pardon, sir, " said Dyke Darrel, "but you are making a foolish mistake. I am a detective——"

"That won't go down. If you attempt to escape I will blow out your brains, " returned the officer, still holding his cocked weapon to the head of Dyke Darrel.

The detective was deeply annoyed at this. On board the train were the remains of the daughter of one of Burlington's most prominent citizens, and Dyke was extremely anxious to meet the friends and explain the situation.

"You may take me at once to the chief of police, " said Dyke Darrel, at length. "I can explain to him, since he knows me. "

Another officer approached, and the first one requested him to handcuff his prisoner.

A hot flush of anger shot to the cheek of the detective.

"This is going too far, " he said in a vexed tone. "If you attempt to put the irons on me, I'll make you trouble. I tell you I am acquainted with your chief, and demand that you take me to him. "

"That's fair enough, " said the second officer.

"But he's a dangerous character, " persisted the first.

"Whom do you take me for, " Dyke demanded indignantly.

"Slim Steve, the train robber. "

"Where did you get your information? "

"It doesn't matter. "

"You'd better go slow, officer. Look at that, and tell me what you think of it? "

Turning back the lap of his coat Dyke Darrel revealed a glittering silver star, and below this a flaming eye on a dark background.

"A Pinkerton detective! " exclaimed the second officer.

"I am a detective, and know my business without receiving instructions from the police of a one-horse town, " retorted Dyke Darrel in anger. "I am willing, however, to visit your chief, who will confirm my words. "

"We had orders from him to arrest you. "

"Very good. I demand that you take me before him. "

After a short consultation the two officers concluded to gratify their prisoner, and, without attempting to handcuff him, they conducted him from the depot to the police station.

As luck would have it, the chief was in, and at once recognized and greeted Dyke Darrel. Explanations soon followed.

"You must not blame my men, " said the chief, "for word was sent from an interior town in Illinois stating that a notorious crook was on the train, and would stop at Burlington. A description was given that tallied with yours, and so the mistake was made. "

"Do you know who sent the dispatch? "

"A sheriff, I think. "

"Just accommodate me with the name of the town, please. "

Dyke Darrel was deeply excited at this last attempt to deprive him of his liberty.

The officer referred to the dispatch and read the name of the place from whence it originated.

"Woodburg! "

Dyke Darrel uttered the name in wonder.

"I don't understand it, " he said; "that is my own home, and I am too well known there to merit suspicion. It must have been meant for a practical joke, " and the detective's thoughts were turned to Harper Elliston.

"It might be, of course, " admitted the chief of Burlington police, "but it is a joke that I shouldn't relish, and you might make it warm for the perpetrator. I can telegraph and inquire into it if you wish, Mr. Darrel. "

"Not now. I shall be in Woodburg within a few days, and then I will find out all about it. "

Dyke Darrel repaired at once to the home of Captain Osborne, which was occupied by relatives of the Captain, and informed them of the sad fate that had overtaken Sibyl Osborne.

An aunt and cousin, the latter a young man of prominence, were the relatives mentioned. The cousin promised to attend the remains, after listening to the strange story Dyke Darrel had to tell. Sibyl had left home ten days before, pretending to go on a visit to friends. When she left it was not suspected that she was out of her mind, consequently the news was all the more sad.

From Burlington the railroad detective returned to Black Hollow, and from there he went to St. Louis to consult with Harry Bernard. Here he was met with the announcement that his young friend had taken the train for Chicago some days before.

This was an annoying state of affairs indeed.

Remaining a few days in St. Louis, Dyke Darrel at length left the city en route for Woodburg. He was anxious to meet Nell, from whom he had been absent now about a fortnight.

On reaching Woodburg the detective found a telegram awaiting him from Chicago:

"Come at once. I have made an important discovery.

"H. "

Of course this must be from Harry. It was dated some days before, however, which annoyed Dyke. Harry Bernard might have changed his base of operations by this time.

"I will call at the house, " mused Dyke Darrel. "I have an hour's time before the next Chicago train. "

Aunt Jule was extremely glad to meet "Marse Dyke. "

"Why didn't you bring the young missus wid yo? " questioned the negress.

"What's that? Hope you didn't think I'd committed matrimony? " and the detective laughed lightly, at the same time chucking Aunt Jule under her fat chin.

"Lor-a-massy, no, Marse Dyke. I meant Missy Nell, " explained the black woman.

"Miss Nell? Isn't she at home? "

"Wal, now, what a question. In coorse she ain't. Didn' yo' send fur her yo' very self? How den yo' 'spec she's goin' to be home ef yo' didn' done brung her, eh? "

All this was Greek to Dyke Darrel.

"What in the name of caution are you driving at, Aunt Jule? I haven't seen my sister since I left home, and if she's gone to look for me she's done a very foolish thing, for I'm not long in one place—she ought to have known better. "

Aunt Jule flounced out of the room, to return soon with a yellow envelope in her hand.

"Dere, look a-dat now. Ef yo' didn' done writ dat, den I'd like to know who did. "

The detective opened the letter his housekeeper placed in his hand, and read:

"CHICAGO, April 30, 188-.

NELL: —Come on the next train, as I wish to see you in this city. Aunt Jule will look after the house until your return. Don't disappoint me. "DYKE. "

The detective glanced at the negress after reading this note, the writing of which very much resembled his hand.

"This came when? "

"Yesterday. "

"Through the mail? "

"Yes, Marse. "

A frown darkened the brow of the detective. He crumpled the letter in his hand and began pacing the floor with nervous strides.

"Somefin must be wrong ef yo' didn' write that letter. "

Suddenly Dyke Darrel turned on the speaker and touched her huge arm with a clinging hand.

"Jule, when did my sister answer this letter? " he demanded, fiercely.

"Jest the next train. "

"Last night? "

"Yes, Marse Dyke. "

Dropping his hand from Aunt Jule's huge arm, the detective rushed from the room and the house. He was laboring under great excitement, as well he might be, for Nell was as the apple of his eye, and she had been enticed to the great city for a fell purpose, he believed.

CHAPTER XVII

NELL IN THE TOILS.

The instant after Professor Ruggles fired, the masked face in the doorway disappeared, and the sound of swift-moving feet was heard.

Still clutching his weapon, the Professor strode to the door and flung it open, gazing into the alley, which framed no reply to the question that trembled unspoken on his lips.

"Did you hit him, Professor? "

"I fear I didn't. "

Professor Ruggles then made an examination of the alley that assured him that his bullet had not been stopped by flesh and bone—instead, it lay on the ground where it had fallen, flattened, from the brick wall above.

"So much for being a poor shot, " sneered the woman.

"So much for your condemned carelessness in not locking the door, " he retorted with equal severity.

"Well, maybe you'd better see that it is fastened now. "

Professor Darlington Ruggles turned the key in the lock, and then assumed a seat once more.

"Let me see. Where did we leave off? "

"In a mighty important place, " answered the woman. "If that sneak had been at the door long, he must have heard something of our plans. "

"And it makes you feel uneasy? "

"Don't it you? "

"A trifle. I can't imagine who the sneak was. "

"Nor I. "

"It might have been one of the boys playing a joke, " said Ruggles.

"I hope it's nothing more serious. "

"I shall dismiss the sneak from my mind at any rate, " returned Mr. Ruggles. "To-morrow night you may look for your guest, Mrs. Scarlet. Remember, whatever plans for vengeance you may have formed will be more than gratified in placing this detective's sister completely in the power of a man who knows how to use it. "

The Professor's eyes snapped at the last, and he lifted and smoothed his hat rapidly with one long arm.

"I understand. Nothing can be too harsh and awful for one of the breed, " hissed Madge Scarlet, in a way that made even Professor Ruggles' flesh creep.

Then he rose to go.

"I will see you again ere long. "

Mrs. Scarlet locked the door after the retreating form of the tall Professor, and then, going to the little table, she sat down, and resting her thin cheeks between her hands, she cried:

"It is coming, it is coming! At last I am to avenge the insults heaped upon me and mine by that scoundrel, who sends men to prison for money, for pay doled out to him by the minions of the law. Dan'l, if you can look down on your old widow to-night, from your home among the stars, you will see her with tears of joy in her old eyes at thought of how she will avenge herself on your enemies. When once that girl comes into my hands, I will execute vengeance to suit myself, without regard to Professor Ruggles, or any other man. "

So it would seem that even the Professor did not fully comprehend the depth of Mrs. Scarlet's vindictiveness toward Dyke Darrel.

It was Professor Darlington Ruggles who penned the letter to Nell Darrel that sent the unsuspecting girl to Chicago to meet her brother.

She was not a little surprised at not finding Dyke at the depot to meet her, and consequently felt a thrill of alarm at seeing so many strange faces.

Why had he not come?

While standing meditating on what course to pursue, a gentleman in rather seedy garments, yet withal not bad looking, stepped up and touched the girl's arm.

"Is this Miss Darrel? "

"Yes, sir, " answered the girl, promptly, at the same time regarding the tall, sunset-haired gentleman, who bowed and lifted his tall hat, with no little curiosity.

"I am Oscar Sims, a friend to the great detective, and ever ready to serve his handsome sister. "

"But, sir, I do not think that it will be at all necessary. I expect my brother at any minute, now, " returned Nell, with a cool hauteur, meant to be freezing.

Nell had heard of the villainous sharks of the great city, who lie in wait for unsuspecting maidens, and she did not mean to be taken in by one of them. Mr. Sims, however, seemed to be a kind gentleman, and when he looked hurt at her remark she hastened to apologize for seeming rudeness.

"It is not at all necessary, " said Mr. Sims, with a bland smile. "Mr. Darrel requested me to visit the depot, and look after a young lady whom he expected on the evening train from Woodburg. I hope you will not distrust one who has the best interests of the great detective at heart. "

Again the red-haired gentleman bowed, and looked smilingly into the face of the young girl.

For the time, Nell was thrown off her guard.

"I—I expected to meet my brother, " she articulated. "He said nothing about you—a stranger—meeting me at the depot. "

"No; and good reason why. He did not know when he wrote that it would be impossible for him to get to the depot. A slight accident— —"

"Accident! Dyke injured? Then let me go to him at once, " cried the impulsive girl, before the man could complete his sentence.

"It is not so very bad, " said Mr. Sims, as he led the way to the walk without, and placed his fair charge on the cushions of a hack. Giving low instructions to the driver, he vaulted to the side of Nell Darrel, and the hack rattled away.

Nell sat flushed and silent for some minutes, her heart throbbing painfully.

"Tell me about it, " she finally said to her companion. "How did it happen? "

"I can't give you the particulars, since they were not given to me, " answered he. "I only know that Dyke met with a fall on the stone pavement, and Dr. Boneset says that his leg is broken. He is in considerable pain, but cheerful withal, and will be mighty glad to see Nell, as he calls you. "

Again the man smiled in the face of the girl at his side, and up to this time no suspicion of the truth flashed upon her brain.

Although the hack moved rapidly, it seemed to the anxious girl a long time in reaching its destination.

"Mr. Darrel is at my house, " said the gentleman, "and I live at least two miles from the depot. "

This was said to silence the growing uneasiness manifested by Miss Darrel.

When at length the hack came to a halt, Mr. Sims quickly alighted and lifted Nell Darrel to the curb; then the hack sped swiftly into the night.

Nell gazed about her with a shudder.

The low, dingy buildings and bad smell pervading the place startled her.

"It cannot be that this is the place, " she cried, standing firm, as he attempted to lead her toward a door, over which glimmered a faint light.

"Oh, yes it is. "

"But I will not go in there. "

"We'll see about that, " he growled, suddenly lifting her in his arms and striding forward.

CHAPTER XVIII.

BEATEN BACK.

The moment Nell Darrel felt herself lifted from her feet she uttered a wild cry, which was smothered in its inception by the hand of her captor.

"Quiet, child; nobody's going to hurt you if you behave yourself. "

Nell was young and vigorous, and she made a desperate struggle for liberty. It was with the utmost difficulty that the man made his way to the room occupied by Mrs. Scarlet.

"Bring the chloroform, " said the villain. "We can't do anything with the girl without it. "

"I'll fix her! " answered the woman, in a voice that sent a shudder to the heart of poor Nell.

Then a subtle fume filled the girl's nostrils, and soon her senses faded out upon a sea of nothingness—her troubles were over for the time.

Then the man, who was none other than Professor Ruggles, bore his insensible burden after the steps of Mrs. Scarlet, to a room in a gloomy basement beneath the building.

As we have before remarked, it was in a disreputable part of the city, and it was not likely that the friends of the fair Nell would look in such a quarter for her.

"Now, then, " said Professor Ruggles, when the twain were once more in the room above, "I shall hold you responsible for the girl's safe keeping, Mrs. Scarlet. "

"I'm ready to do my part, " answered the woman. "How long will you keep her here? "

"As long as suits my purpose. I am not sure. I may conclude to wait until Dyke Darrel is put off the trail before I take the girl to Gotham;

that city will be my ultimate destination. I must leave you now, my dear, but I shall call to-morrow and see how my girl is getting on. "

He turned then as if about to depart.

"See here Professor! "

"Eh? "

He faced about once more.

"Haven't you forgotten something? "

"I think not. "

"The girl must eat! "

"Certainly. "

"And do you imagine *I* am going to pay the bill? " demanded the woman, tartly.

"Well, I had forgotten that a little of the root of evil was necessary in your case. "

A smile, deepening into a disagreeable laugh, followed, as Professor Ruggles laid a greenback in the hand of his tool.

A moment later he was gone.

As the door closed on his retreating form, the countenance of Madge Scarlet underwent a change. The wrinkled face flushed with wrath, and the skinny hands were raised on high.

"Professor Ruggles, you may have successfully duped the girl, but you cannot make one of me. I can read you like a book, and it maybe that I shall conclude not to permit you to have your way in this matter. Through this girl I shall be able to wring the heart of the man I hate, and I mean to do it. Ah! Dyke Darrel, venomous scoundrel! The hour of my revenge draws nigh! I shall willingly cast my soul into Hades for this one drop of satisfaction. "

There was an awful glitter in the woman's eyes at the last, and her fierce emotions caused her frame to tremble visibly.

In the meantime, how fared it with poor Nell Darrel, who had gone thus blindly to her doom? She did not awake from the stupor caused by the chloroform, until another day had dawned upon the world, although but little light was permitted to find its way into this underground apartment, whose stone walls were damp with ooze, and from whence no voice could penetrate to the busy world above.

A faint light entered the place from between iron bars that spanned a narrow window, far above the head of little Nell Darrel.

The only furniture in this cellar was a straw cot, on which Nell had been laid, and a low stool. The girl felt terribly sick and weak when she came to realize her condition.

She could understand now the truth, when too late, that she had been enticed from home by a villain, and naturally enough her thoughts reverted to Harper Elliston.

Yet, why should she think of that man? Surely he was not wicked enough to stoop to anything of this kind.

Nell was not to be left long in suspense, however. The door to her prison creaked on its hinges, and a man entered and stood confronting her in the gray light.

It was Harper Elliston.

There was a smile on his sinister countenance, and he stroked his beard with the coolest insolence imaginable.

"How do you find yourself this morning, my dear? " questioned Elliston in a low voice.

"This is your work, villain! "

"Hush; don't speak in such a harsh tone, Nell, " answered Mr. Elliston, with a deprecatory wave of the hand. "I cannot permit you to impugn my motive, Miss Darrel. I claim that all is fair in love and war. You know from repeated assurances on my part that I love you; once I wished to make you my wife. Blame me not if I have changed my mind on that score; it is you who have driven me to it. Nevertheless, I am constrained to deal justly and kindly with you, my girl, and again offer to share my New York palace with you. Could anything be more generous? "

The infamy of his proposition roused all the fire in the nature of Nell Darrel.

"Harper Elliston, how dare you insult me in this way? Do you imagine that I would for one moment countenance anything so base? You have missed your mark if you imagine you can frighten me into consenting to my own ruin. "

"It may be accomplished without your consent. "

Such a look as swept his face startled the girl. The hideous nature of the man was now revealed in all its naked deformity. She shrank from him as she would have shrunk from a venomous serpent.

He continued to smile and stroke his glossy beard.

"You see how it is, my dear, " he proceeded. "The wisest thing you can do is to submit to the inevitable. "

He advanced as lie spoke.

She recoiled with a shudder of wild alarm.

"Back, scoundrel! Do not touch me! " she cried, warningly, an indignant, perhaps dangerous, fire blazing in her eye.

Again the demon laughed.

"You seem to take my love-making hard, Miss Darrel. "

"Not another step, " warned Nell.

"Ho! ho! ho! Would you try to frighten me? You can't do that, I've tamed more than one such as you. Come, be sensible, and let me have one kiss at least. "

Again he advanced.

CLICK!

Harper Elliston uttered a low yet startled cry and shrank back in alarm.

A cocked derringer gleamed in the hand of Nell Darrel, and the open muzzle was pointed at his breast.

This was as disagreeable as it was unexpected.

A low-muttered oath fell from the lips of the baffled villain.

"Girl, have a care, that weapon may go off, " he cried, in a voice husky with disappointment and rage.

"It WILL go off if you do not depart at once, " she answered, with all the sternness she was able to muster.

"Hand that pistol to me. "

"Never! Its contents you will get if you dare advance another step. "

Harper Elliston realized that he was baffled for the present. He had never suspected the presence of a weapon on the person of Nell Darrel, else he would have disarmed her at the outset.

After a moment of hesitancy the villain turned and strode from the place. When Nell attempted to follow she was confronted by a solid oak door that Elliston had quickly closed and locked behind him.

With a low moan Nell retreated and sank weak and trembling on the miserable cot, and for the next few minutes gave free rein to her alarm in tears.

In the meantime Elliston hurried above, and confronted Madge Scarlet with a terrible frown on his brow.

"You and that red-headed Professor have played a smart trick on me, old woman, a mighty smart trick; but let me tell you it won't go down for a cent. I don't like it much, neither. "

"Eh? I don't understand, " said Mrs. Scarlet.

"I'll make you understand, " and Elliston advanced angrily upon the woman, and raised his hand.

"Strike if you dare! "

She looked ugly at that moment.

"You're just capable of strikin' a woman, " sneered Madge Scarlet. "I've seen such critters before. God never meant them for men, however. "

Mr. Elliston held his hand. He saw that he had come near making a mistake.

"Forgive me, Mrs. Scarlet, " he said in a subdued voice. "I was beside myself, but I had reason to be. Do you know that Nell Darrel is armed? "

"No. "

"She IS, nevertheless, with a pistol. She's a perfect tigress, and would as soon shoot me as not. I shall leave it for you to get the weapon from her. "

"I can do it easy enough. "

"I hope so. To-night I will have more definite plans. I may conclude to take the girl away then. "

Mr. Elliston passed from the room. He had been gone but a few minutes when another person entered—Nick Brower, the tool and friend of Mrs. Scarlet and the Professor.

"Well, what's the news, Nick. My nephew is still in durance vile? "

"Yes, " answered the low ruffian, "and what's more, Dyke Darrel, the detective, is in Chicago! "

CHAPTER XIX.

THE DETECTIVE FOOLED.

Two men met unexpectedly in one of the hotel corridors of the great city; two hands went out, and

"How are you, Harry? "

"How are you, Dyke, old boy? "

"When did you leave St. Louis? "

This from the detective.

"Not long since. I am confident that our game is in this vicinity. I meant to come down to Woodburg soon, and consult with you. I sent a telegram, but it brought no answer from you. "

"I wasn't at home. It was placed in my hands yesterday. "

"And that is why you are here? "

"Not wholly. "

There was a gloomy look on the face of the detective, not natural to it, and young Bernard knew that something had gone decidedly wrong with his detective friend.

"It is about Nell, " said Dyke Darrel, when questioned. "She came to the city last evening, in answer to a letter purporting to come from me. The letter was a decoy from some villain, and I fear that Nell has met with a terrible fate. "

A groan came at the last.

Harry Bernard's face blanched, and he, too, seemed excited and deeply moved. The keen eyes of Dyke Darrel noticed the young man's emotion, and he felt a suspicion growing stronger each moment.

"Nell in the city—decoyed! " exclaimed Harry at length. "Great heaven! Dyke, this is awful! " "It is. "

Then the detective laid his hand on the young man's shoulder, and piercing him with a stern look, said in an awful voice:

"Harry Bernard, on your honor as a man, what do you know of this enticing of Nell to the city? "

"What do I know? "

"Yes; what do you know? "

There was a stern ring in the detective's voice, not to be mistaken.

"I know only what you have just told me, Dyke. "

"This is the truth? "

"Good heaven! Dyke Darrel, do you imagine that *I* had aught to do with enticing your sister to this wicked city? My soul! You do not understand the feeling that animates my heart for Nell Darrel. I hope you will not insult me again with a suspicion so haggard and awful."

The hurt look resting on the face of the young amateur detective was sufficient to convince Dyke Darrel that Harry Bernard spoke the truth, and this knowledge only increased his uneasiness.

"I am fearful some terrible ill has befallen Nell, " groaned Dyke.

"My friend, " said Harry, "we must let all other matters rest until we find the girl. I have a suspicion that may lead to something definite. Let me tell you now, that during the past year you have warmed a serpent in your bosom in the person of Harper Elliston. I have never, until now, dared make this assertion in your presence, knowing as I did the great respect you had for the oily-tongued fellow. The time for plain speaking has come, however. "

"I shall take no offense. "

"No! I am glad to hear you say that. Come to my room, Dyke, and I will tell you something that may open your eyes a little. "

The detective complied, and when they were seated Harry poured out his confidence.

"I am glad you have been thus frank with me, Harry, " said the detective when his friend had finished. "I have heard enough of late to convince me that Elliston is a wolf in sheep's clothing! "

"And that is one point gained. "

"It is. "

"And I believe that it was Elliston who penned the decoy letter. "

"I am more than half convinced that such is the case, " admitted Dyke Darrel.

"Have you investigated? "

"Thoroughly, since I came into town. I learned that Nell got off at the depot, and that she met a red-haired man, and entered a hack with him. After that all is blank. "

"That confirms my suspicions, Dyke. " "What is that? "

This man with the florid looks meeting Nell, and going away from the depot in her company, Professor Ruggles, is a friend of Elliston's."

"Indeed! "

"It is true. I believe before another day passes, the place of the girl's seclusion can be found. Down on Clark street is Mother Scarlet's place, a played-out old hag, and she has been hand and glove with this red-haired man for some time. "

"Mother Scarlet! " exclaimed the detective. "I have met her; she is the aunt of the Martin Skidway who is now serving out the remainder of his term for counterfeiting. "

"The same, I suppose. I move that we visit her den, and see what we can find. "

"Agreed. Let us go at once. "

Dyke Darrel came to his feet.

"One moment, Dyke. "

"Well. "

"You are too well known by the crooks of this city to move about without disguise. "

"I will fix that. I will meet you again in an hour. "

And then Dyke Darrel hurried away.

It was almost dark when two men, one old and gray, with a hump on his shoulder, called at a dingy old brick on Clark street and rapped on a narrow door that opened into an alley.

No answer was vouchsafed.

Then the old man turned the knob, but the door refused to yield.

"What's wanted, you fellers? "

The voice came from behind the two men. Turning, they saw a stout, ill-looking fellow, with unkempt hair and beard, peering in at them from the street.

"Ain't this the house where Mrs. Scarlet stops, " questioned the elderly man.

"Mebbe 'tis. "

"Where's the woman now? "

"Bless your soul, old man, I don't know. Better call agin; she's allus in evenings, " suggested the man at the edge of the street.

"Mebbe we had, " grunted the old man at the door. Then he and his companion moved out of the alley. They went but a little way when they came to a full stop, and entered into a low confab.

A pair of keen eyes was watching them during the time, however, and a little later the man who had addressed the two strangers walked away. He passed to the rear of the block, and made his way by a back stairs to a room on the first floor. Here he found the one he was seeking— Mrs. Scarlet—who was engaged in discussing a supper of bread and beer.

She was alone.

"Eh? so you're here again, Nick? Did he send ye? "

"The Professor? "

"Who else should I mean? "

"Wall, he didn't, then. I seed a couple of blokes in the alley jist now, and they 'quired for you. "

"Why didn't you send 'em up? " and the woman laughed in a way that revealed her ragged teeth and unwholesome gums.

"They'll be back soon 'nough, " answered the man. "I've an idee they mean mischief. Better you go below and see 'em when they do come."

"All right. "

About an hour after darkness had settled, while Madge Scarlet sat in the lower room, the one in which we have so many times met her, the door was unceremoniously opened, and a man crossed the threshold.

An old man he was, with bent form and white hair, a hump disfiguring his shoulder, his trembling right hand resting on the top of a cane.

"Good evening, mistress. "

The old man, who had closed the door sharply to behind him, sank to a rickety chair as he uttered the greeting.

"I don't know you, " retorted Madge Scarlet sharply. "Haven't you got into the wrong house? "

"Well, I dunno, " whined the man in a sharp falsetto voice. "I reckon if you're Mistress Scarlet, you're the one I'm to see. "

"I'm not ashamed to own to the name, old man. Let's have your business at once. "

"I'm pretty much broke up since I came out of the bastile, " said the old man. "'Taint jest the place for a gentleman, I can tell you that. It's mighty down-settin' on one's pride, which I had a heap of afore I was sent to abide there. "

"Who are you and what are you driving at? "

Mrs. Scarlet asked the question with a puzzled stare. She was possessed of a very suspicious nature, and she was not ready to accept a person on outward appearance alone.

"I'm William Sugg, from Missoury, " the old man answered promptly. "I came all the way to Shecargo to see the aunt of a friend. Mebbe you'll understand when I tell you, that Martin Skidway was one of the best friends an old man like me had in the bastile. "

The name of her nephew opened the way to Madge Scarlet's heart at once.

She questioned Mr. Sugg about the young man, and he answered her with the assurance that they had been inmates of the same prison, and that Martin was losing flesh rapidly from melancholy.

"It's the doings of that devil, Dyke Darrel, " cried Mrs. Scarlet, losing her temper at thought of her troubles.

"I've kind o' thought, bein' as I was in Shecargy, I'd look up a boardin' place and stay a spell. I've heerd that you have rooms to rent? "

"I have, to the right ones. "

"Will you show me some? "

"Certainly. "

Mrs. Scarlet rose and lifted a lamp from the table.

"Come this way. "

As the woman led the way through a back door, into another apartment, a pair of strong hands suddenly seized and held her fast, while a voice hissed in her ear:

"Not a sound or you die! "

It was a startling situation.

"I am here for a purpose, " said the old man, a sudden change in his voice. "I want you to lead me to the room in which Nell Darrel is confined. "

The man's hands fell from the woman's shoulders, and when she turned about, she found that he had her covered with a revolver.

His voice sounded familiar.

"You're the detective, Dyke Darrel? "

"It matters not. Show me the way to the room where you have Nell Darrel imprisoned, " uttered the man in a stern voice.

The menacing revolver decided the woman. The old building had been arranged for emergencies of this kind, as the sequel will show. A strange glitter came to the eyes of Mrs. Scarlet as she said:

"Who told you that Nell Darrel was in this house? "

"It matters not. Lead the way at once, or it will be the worse for you."

"You dare not harm me. "

"I'll show you, if you attempt to play me false. A dozen policemen have their eyes on this building at this moment. "

"Come on. "

The woman turned and walked forward. She passed into a hall, and halting at a side door, unlocked it and pushed it open.

"In there. "

"Go on. You shall keep me company. "

Mrs. Scarlet advanced, closely followed by the detective.

The moment he crossed the threshold the door closed behind him, and the lamp was extinguished, leaving everything in total darkness. Then the detective felt the floor give way, and he was precipitated to his doom, the last sound reaching his ears being a mocking laugh from Aunt Scarlet.

CHAPTER XX.

OVERMATCHED BY A GIRL.

A low chuckle fell from the lips of Madge Scarlet.

"I reckon you've met your match this time, Dyke Darrel. I will now enjoy the sweetest revenge; it will be like honey to my blistered tongue. You've done your last shadowing of your betters. Dan'l, husband, you shall be avenged before to-morrow's sun rises over Chicago. "

Lighting her lamp, the woman fiend bent down and peered through a square opening in the floor to the depths below. It was too far down for the rays of light to penetrate, but she could well imagine that a mangled form lay directly below on the stone floor.

A faint groan reached her ears.

"Ha! he's coming to his senses. I must see that he don't outwit Aunt Madge yet. "

Then replacing the trap, the woman left the place, and a little later descended a narrow stairs and entered the room beneath the trap.

There on the stone floor lay the pretended old man, gasping in pain, yet not able to help himself.

Quickly Madge Scarlet bent over the prostrate and helpless victim of her cunning, and began binding his limbs with a stout cord that she had brought with her for the purpose.

In a little time the work was completed, and Mrs. Scarlet stood up with her arms akimbo viewing her work, a satisfied smile playing about the toothless lips.

"I'll peel you, so't there'll be no deception hereafter, " muttered the she fiend; and suiting actions to words, she tore the disguise from the detective's head and face and flung it aside. "Thought to fool the old woman, eh? "

A curdling laugh followed.

After gloating over the detective for some time, Madge Scarlet picked up her lamp and turned away, a feeling of intense satisfaction in her heart at the knowledge that she had her enemies so completely at her mercy. It was satisfaction for one day at least.

The woman passed through two basement rooms, unlocking and locking doors, until she at length stood in the presence of Nell Darrel. "I ain't here with supper, madam, " sneered the woman, as Nell started up and approached her. "You're not to have a mouthful to eat jest at present; that's the compliments your husband sends. "

But Nell did not seem to appreciate the gross wit of her keeper.

"I am not hungry, woman, but I appeal to you to permit me to go from this place. I shall die here in a short time. "

"Die then! Nothing would please me better than to witness your last struggles, " and Mrs. Scarlet emitted a laugh that was horrible to hear.

Nell had much of the determined spirit of her daring brother in her composition. She was not yet ready to give up all hope and fall crushed in despair. Her right hand grasped the butt of the little derringer she had been thoughtful enough to provide herself with before leaving home.

"Will nothing move you, woman? "

"Nothing, " sneered Mrs. Scarlet. "Your brother sent my husband to a dungeon, and to his death, and for that and other wicked work of his, I mean to be avenged. I shall cause him to suffer through his sister. You imagine the handsome Elliston a monster, I reckon, but I will show you that he is but a child compared to Madge Scarlet. "

"Stop; I do not care to listen to you. Please hand over the keys to this den of demons. "

A cocked pistol was brought forward to emphasize the fair prisoner's demand.

A sneering laugh answered the girl's demand. Madge Scarlet did not seem to look upon the weapon as a dangerous one.

"Quick! I have no time to parley. Fling down the keys—toss them to the door yonder, then take your place in yonder corner. Do you hear me? "

So stern was the girl's voice, so full of intense meaning, as to amaze the infamous woman who confronted her.

"This is all a joke——. "

"It will prove a dear joke to you if you don't obey. Stop. One step toward me and I fire! I am in deadly earnest. "

And the sneering Madge Scarlet realized that she was. It was a most humiliating position. Once the woman thought of making a quick spring, but a pressure of the trigger was all that was necessary to send a bullet on an errand of death.

With reluctance the woman drew a bundle of keys from her pocket and flung them to the floor behind her, and close to the door that stood ajar.

"Don't be so spiteful. Now, then, go to that corner. Move quickly! "

The girl still threatened her keeper with the cocked derringer, and she crossed the floor with a growl that was not pleasant to hear.

"There, that is about right. "

Then Nell Darrel backed to the door, snatched up the bunch of keys and lamp, passed into the next room, securing the door just as the hag from within came against it with tremendous force, at the same time uttering a series of the most ear-splitting yells.

The door failed to yield, and Nell now hastened to improve her opportunity for escape that the carelessness of Mrs. Scarlet had given her.

CHAPTER XXI.

A BOUT IN THE CELLAR.

It was a stout tin lamp that the fleeing girl held in her hand, and the blaze filled the subterranean apartment but dimly.

She found herself in a square room, larger than the one she had just left. Advancing to a door she tried it, to find it locked. This was made to yield, however, by one of the bunch of keys, and she proceeded to another door that stood ajar.

"Help! "

It was a smothered cry that reached the girl's ears, and quite startled her.

The sound came from the next apartment. For a minute Nell Darrel hesitated. She reasoned that she had nothing to fear from the hag who kept the place, and one who was in need of help certainly could not be a friend to Mrs. Scarlet, or those who profited by the old woman's villainy.

"Help! "

Again came that cry, and Nell moved forward, pushed open the door and flashed her light over the scene—a room much smaller than the one she had just quitted.

A dark object writhing on the floor startled her vision.

"Old woman, do you mean to murder me here? "

The man seemed to imagine that the new comer was the hag who kept the place. With trembling step Nell Darrel advanced and flashed her light into the face of a bound and helpless prisoner.

"Mercy! It is Dyke! "

Stunned at the discovery, Nell was completely overcome for the time, and stood with arms extended like one petrified.

"Nell, is it you? " cried the yet stunned detective. "Where is the old hag who rules this den of iniquity? "

"Back yonder, safely locked in a room, " said Nell, when she could find voice.

"And you did it? "

"Yes. "

"Cut these cords, brave girl, and we will soon be out of this. "

Placing her lamp on a box near, Nell Darrel proceeded to comply with the request of her brother. She had with her a small open knife, and this came into play neatly enough.

Soon the detective's limbs were free. He found when he attempted to rise, that he was unable to do so.

"I received a bad fall, " he said, with a groan. "Lend me a hand, Nell, and we will get out of this before friends of that woman come to her rescue. "

Nell assisted her brother to his feet. He groaned with pain, for it seemed to him as though every bone in his body was broken.

"I was a fool to run into such a trap, " he muttered.

"Can you walk, brother? "

"I can make a desperate try at any rate, " uttered the detective, grimly. Then, assisted by Nell's arm, he hobbled across the floor toward a narrow stairs that promised them passage to rooms above.

The beard and wig were left in the cellar.

The sound of steps on the floor overhead brought brother and sister to a sudden halt.

"Hark! "

"Some one is coming, " uttered Nell.

"It seems so. "

Then the sound of an opening door startled them.

"It's strange that Madge has left everything in such a careless way, " said a masculine voice. "Ho! Madge, where are you? "

"Hold up thar, " uttered another voice. "I reckin the old gal know'd what she was doin'. Thar's some skulduggery goin' on down here, or my name ain't Nick Brower. I seed an old bloke come in, and 'twixt me an you, Professor, it was the man you'n me would give more to see out of the world than in it. "

"You mean Dyke Darrel, the detective? "

"I couldn't mean anybody else. "

"Come on, then, let's investigate. "

"Extinguish your light, Nell, " cried Dyke Darrel, in a thrilling whisper.

The girl did so at once, but the men above flashed a light into the basement room, and soon steps were heard descending the stairs. Dyke felt over his person to discover that Mother Scarlet had been prudent enough to deprive him of arms.

Nell, white as death, yet with a determined look in her eyes, clinched her derringer firmly, and with close-shut teeth waited the denouement.

"If we could only get under the stairs, " said the detective, in a low voice.

They made a move to carry out his suggestion, but it was too late.

"Ha! "

This exclamation fell from the lips of the foremost man of three who were descending the narrow stairs. The outcry was caused at seeing two forms gliding across the stone floor toward the stairs.

"Quick! Hold up there, or we fire! " cried a sharp voice. Then the three men rapidly descended to the floor and confronted Nell and the detective. Three revolvers were leveled, and death literally stared brother and sister in the face.

"Caught, by the powers, " sneered lips above a massive red beard, and Professor Darlington Ruggles' eyes glittered with intense satisfaction as they peered into the face of the famous railroad detective.

Had Dyke Darrel been in the full vigor of his manly strength, and Nell not by to unnerve him, his chances for escape would have been tenfold greater.

As it was, a terrible weakness oppressed him. His fall into the basement had jarred him terribly, and it was with difficulty that he could stand alone. The walls seemed to whirl about in a mad waltz, and the faces of the three villains seemed one mass of grinning demons.

"Halt! "

Nell Darrel, white as death, yet with the fires of a resolute purpose blazing in her eyes, thrust forward her pistol.

"It's pretty Nell on a lark! " exclaimed Professor Ruggles. "It will be better for you not to make any resistance, for the moment you attempt it, that moment death will come to both of you. Be wise in time. "

The Professor advanced a step.

"Stop there, " sternly ordered the girl.

"Aye! stop there, " repeated Dyke, in a voice husky from very weakness. "We will not be taken alive. Do you know on what dangerous grounds you are treading? This block is surrounded by members of the force, and any harm offered to Nell or myself speedily avenged. "

A jeering laugh answered the detective.

"It is wrong to tell such a whopper, Mr. Darrel, especially when one is on the verge of eternity, " said Ruggles, showing his teeth.

The situation was interesting.

"Will you permit us to depart from here? " questioned the detective, suddenly.

This speech brought a laugh to the lips of Darlington Ruggles.

"You do not seem to know me! " he said.

"I know that you pretend to be a professor of some sort, but I believe that you are in disguise. I think, if you would cast aside that red hirsute covering, we should see — —"

"Zounds! Go for him, boys, " cried Professor Ruggles in a loud voice, completely drowning the faint accents of Dyke Darrel.

The two men who kept the Professor company, made a quick move to seize the twain in front of them. On the instant came a flash and sharp report.

One of the villains staggered and sank with a groan against the stairs.

"I—I'm shot! " he gasped.

"The she jade! "

It was Nick Brower who uttered the hissing cry of rage, and the next instant the villain's revolver flashed.

"My God! You have killed Nell! "

It was a cry expressive of the deepest agony, as the weak and reeling detective caught the form of his sister in his arms, as she fell backward, with the blood streaming down her face.

Poor Nell!

She hung a dead weight in the arms of Dyke Darrel—murdered by the hand of a brutal assassin.

No wonder the bruised and almost helpless man-hunter groaned with inward anguish at the sight.

He fell no easy prey into the hands of his enemies, however.

Staggering backward, and easing his bleeding relative to the ground, he turned with a mad cry and dashed at the throat of Professor Darlington Ruggles.

Both men staggered across the floor against the stairs.

"I will strangle you for this, " hissed the enraged detective.

"Help! " gasped Ruggles.

Brower came to his assistance with a vengeance, and rained terrific blows upon the head of Dyke Darrel with the butt of his revolver. Soon the mad grip relaxed from the throat of Ruggles, and Dyke Darrel sank a bleeding and insensible mass to the floor.

Panting and gasping, Professor Ruggles leaned against the stairs and gazed about him in the gloom.

The lamp had been overturned in the struggle, and at the last, darkness reigned supreme.

"I've fixed him, Professor, " growled Nick Brower, in a savage undertone.

"I hope so, the devil. He went for me with the venom of a tiger. Have you a match? "

"Yes. "

"Let's have a light. I'm afraid you have done a miserable job, Nick. "

Inside of five minutes the overturned lamp was recovered and burning once more. Its rays revealed a ghastly scene. Two forms lay on the floor, Dyke Darrel and Nell, both apparently dead.

Nick's companion, who had screamed so lustily at the fire from Nell Darrel's derringer, still leaned against the stairs seeming little the worse for wear.

"Mike, where are you hit? "

"Don't know. I FELT the bullet goin' through my brains. "

A brief examination showed that the man had only been grazed by the shot from the girl's pistol. When this discovery was made Professor Ruggles became very angry.

"You made more fuss than a man shot through the neck ought to. The girl has been killed in consequence. Hades! this has been a bad evening's work. I would rather have lost a thousand dollars than had Nell Darrel slain. "

"She wan't wuth no sich money, " growled Brower.

"How do you know what she was worth, you miserable brute? " snarled the Professor, in an angry voice. "I take it, that I know more about it than you do. "

"See here, boss, aren't you goin' on a bin run for nothin'? Whar'd you be now if I hadn't gin Dyke Darrel his quietus? Mebbe you'd better thank instead of curse your friend. "

There was a deal of homely sense in the words of burly Nick Brower, and the prince of villains realized it.

"I wanted the girl unharmed, Nick. If she's dead I don't suppose it can be helped, however; she brought her fate upon herself. "

"That she did, Prof. "

Professor Ruggles then proceeded to make an examination of the wound in Nell Darrel's head. He was gratified to discover that the bullet had merely glanced across the girl's skull without making a necessarily dangerous wound.

"I will take the girl out of this while you dispose of the detective, " said Ruggles. "Be sure and fix him so that he will give no trouble in the future. "

"Trust me fur thet, " answered the villain Brower.

Then Professor Ruggles passed up the stairs with Nell Darrel in his arms, just as four men halted at the side door in the alley.

CHAPTER XXII.

THE EMPTY SEAT.

A hand shook the door as Professor Ruggles entered the room. He at once suspected something wrong, but cared only for his own safety, and so did not attempt to warn the inmates of Mrs. Scarlet's den of their danger.

He hurried to the rear of the block, down an upper hall, and as he was passing into an alley down the back stairs, the four men had burst in the side door and rushed into Madge Scarlet's dingy sitting-room.

"The beaks are out in force, it seems, " muttered Ruggles, as he halted for a moment on the ground to rest from his exertion. "I hope Nick and that fool pard of his will finish Dyke Darrel before the cops get onto them. As for me, I shall turn my back on this accursed town the moment I am assured that Nell is out of danger. I will be quite secure in New York, I imagine. "

And the red-haired villain made his escape from that building and, leaving his charge in an out-of-the-way alley, went forth to find a conveyance to take the wounded girl to a more safe retreat. He succeeded in finding a hack that suited his purpose, and with his insensible companion he was driven to another part of the city, on the West Side. Ruggles had more than one resort in the great Western metropolis, and after he had placed Nell in a cozy room, with an old negress to watch over her, he breathed easy once more.

Nell Darrel was badly injured, and for several days she raved in delirium. When she came to her senses she was weak and almost helpless. During all this time the black tool of Darlington Ruggles cared for her in a most kindly manner.

The negress had been instructed to do all in her power for the girl, who, the Professor assured her, was a near relative who was not wholly sound in mind, and this fact, combined with an accident, had brought on the trouble from which she was now suffering.

"Poor little lily, " murmured the negress, in a sympathetic tone, when the girl was able to sit up and look about her.

"Where am I? " demanded Nell.

"Youse in good hands, chile, " answered the black woman. "Your cousin says he'll take you outen dis soon's you can trabbel. "

"My cousin? "

Nell stared at the black, seemingly honest face in wonder. Of a sudden the memory of the adventure in the basement on Clark street came to the girl as a light from a clouded sky. She had indeed been under a cloud for a long time, and had no means of judging of the passage of time.

What had happened during all this while? What fate had been her brother's? A feeling of deepest anxiety filled the girl's breast. Ere she could find voice for more words, however, the door opened and a man entered the room.

A low, alarmed cry fell from the lips of Nell Darrel.

Before her stood Harper Elliston, smiling and plucking at his beard, which was but a mere stubble now, he having shaved since she had met him last.

"Ah, Nell, you are looking bright; I trust that you feel better. You have been very sick. How does your head feel? "

For the first time the girl realized that there was a sore spot under her hair at the side of her head. She touched it with her hand, and seemed surprised.

"You have forgotten, doubtless, " he said. "You were rescued from a band of villains nearly a fortnight since. It seems that one of them must have fired at you, since there was a slight wound where you just put your hand, that was doubtless made by a bullet. "

Nell Darrel was beginning to remember the scene in the cellar.

"I was rescued, you say? Who were the rescuers? "

"Myself among others. I think you may safely acknowledge that you owe your life to me, " said the New Yorker coolly.

"And Dyke? " questioned Nell with intense eagerness.

"Was saved also, but he is badly hurt, and will be laid up for a month or more. He is in one of the city hospitals. "

"Oh, sir, I am thankful it is no worse. What have they done with the villains, that sleek one with the red hair and beard? "

"They are all in prison, and will be brought to court as soon as the witnesses are in a condition to appear against them. "

"The witnesses? "

"Dyke Darrel and yourself. "

"Can I go to Dyke? "

"Hardly, " he answered with a smile. "You could not walk, that is certain, and I am sure to attempt to ride would prove a dangerous experiment. I am too deeply interested in your welfare to permit the attempt. "

"But I am quite strong, I assure you, " returned Nell, rising to her feet only to sink back again with a cry of piteous weakness.

"You see, it would not do to attempt leaving your room at present, " said the villain, still smiling. Besides, there is no need of it. Your brother is doing as well as could be expected, and he has the assurance that you are out of danger, which has proved a great comfort to him, I assure you.

"Well, I suppose I ought to be thankful, " sighed Nell, with tears in her dark eyes. "I cannot understand it all just now. It seems strange that I should be subject to such treatment. Do you know the man Sims? "

"Sims? "

"The one with the red beard and hair. He met me at the depot. "

"Exactly. I cannot say that I know the fellow, but I suspect he is a scoundrel of the first water. Don't bother your head about these things now, Nell. Try and get rested and strong, so that you can get from here and back to your own home as soon as possible. I hope you do not fear to trust me? "

He eyed her keenly at the last.

She was too weak to fully realize the enormity of this man's offense. She knew nothing of his connection with, the ruffians who made of Mrs. Scarlet's building a rendezvous; she only knew that he had been indiscreet and insulting once, when in liquor, but of this he might have repented long since. At any rate, he seemed to be doing her a good turn now, and she could do no other way than trust him.

"I am still puzzled about one thing, " she said, seeming to forget the question he had propounded.

"What is that? " asked Elliston.

"Why was I brought here? "

"Simply because you were not able to be taken home. "

"But the hospital——"

"Was no place for a lady. I realized that you needed the best of care, and knowing Aunt Venus was a kind, motherly soul, an excellent nurse, even though she had a black skin, I brought you here. "

"And here I've been—how long? "

"About fourteen days. "

"So long? '

"You are surprised? "

"It doesn't seem a day. "

"I suppose not. You haven't been in your right mind any of the time. Have you any word to send to Dyke? "

"Are you going to him soon? "

"Immediately. I call at the hospital every day to inquire after the dear boy, and I haven't been there this morning. "

His voice was gentle, and there was a moist light in his dark eyes. It was barely possible that she had wronged the New Yorker, and the thought caused a pang. In the time to come she would confess her obligations, but now she was not in a mood for it.

"If I could write a line it would do him more good than aught else, " said Nell.

"Can you control your hand? "

"Oh, yes, easily. "

"Then you shall write the dear boy. As you say, it will be of immense benefit to him. "

Mr. Elliston drew forth from an inner pocket a book. Opening it he tore out a leaf and placed it, with pencil, in the lap of the invalid girl. It was not without difficulty that she controlled her hand sufficiently to write.

Taking the folded note Elliston bade her good morning and passed from the room. The moment he gained the street he tore the bit of paper to fragments, a smile glinting over his face meantime.

"So much for that, " he muttered. "Nell is about in the right trim for removal, and I must not delay another day. Simple little thing! She believed every word that I told her regarding the outcome of that racket on Clark street. What an opinion she would have of me if she knew the exact truth. I must get me to Gotham immediately. My funds are running low, and SHE must replenish them. I haven't seen Aunt Scarlet since the racket. I hope she got her quietus. I believe I have had quite enough of her disinterested assistance; quite enough of it. "

And yet the scheming gentleman was to receive more of the Clark street hag's assistance in the future, and in a way that was not just exactly pleasant, than he imagined.

****

Night hung its sable mantle over the earth. A silver moon rode in a clear sky, and the lightning express rattled down through the night with a hiss and screech that rent the silence with an uncanny sound.

The train was speeding through the Empire State, and when morning dawned, with no accident happening, it would come thundering into the great city by the sea.

Two persons occupying a seat in the car next the sleeper merit our attention. One is a heavily-veiled lady, apparently sleeping, since her head reclines against the back of the seat, and a low breathing is heard, or might be but for the noise made by the train rattling over the steel rails.

Who is the woman?

No need to ask when we note the fact that the man sitting there possesses red hair and beard—the irrepressible Professor Darlington Ruggles, of Chicago. He has been eminently successful thus far in his plot for the safe abduction of Nell Darrel. Under the influence of a powerful drug he conveyed her to the station, and set out on the previous day for the East.

His companion was an invalid sister, who was in a comatose state a portion of the time as the result of her ill health. This was the story told by the Professor to inquisitive people, and the truth did not come to the surface. Travelers, who become accustomed to seeing all sorts of people, are not often suspicious.

The villain was more successful than he could have hoped. Within a few hours he would be in New York, and then he felt that he could bid defiance to pursuit.

It was now past midnight. The man from Chicago felt a deep drowsiness stealing over him. He wished to shake it off, and so, rising and seeing only people in an unconscious state about him, he concluded to go into the smoking-car and enjoy a cigar. He began to feel nervous, and such a stimulant seemed absolutely necessary.

The train drew into a station, paused less than a minute, and then went swiftly on its way.

Calmly the scheming villain sat and puffed at his cigar until it was more than half consumed, then he tossed the stump through the open window, and once more he passed into the other car.

When he gained the seat he had lately occupied, he could not suppress a cry of startled wonder.

THE SEAT WAS EMPTY!

He had left Nell Darrel there not more than twenty minutes since, drugged into complete insensibility. She could not have gone from the seat of her own volition.

An indefinable thrill of fear stole over the stalwart frame of Professor Darlington Ruggles. He glanced up and down the car; the girl was not in sight. But one person was awake, an old man, who said:

"Lookin' fur the young lady? "

The Professor nodded.

"She got off't last station. " "Got off? How—"

"She had help, of course, " explained the old passenger, quickly.

"Who helped her? " cried Ruggles, in a husky voice.

"An old woman, who got on and off at the last station quick's wink."

CHAPTER XXIII.

DYKE DARREL ON THE TRAIL.

The men who burst into Aunt Scarlet's room on the night that Professor Ruggles departed from the block with Nell Darrel in his arms, were men of determination and friends of the detective, who had gone into the building in the disguise of an old man, for the purpose of investigating.

How the investigation came out the reader has been already informed.

The report of pistols had warned Harry Bernard, the boy Paul Ender, and two officers in their company, that something of an interesting nature was going on in the basement of the Scarlet block.

"Dyke is in difficulty, that is sure, " cried Harry, in an excited voice. "We must get inside at once. "

They tried the side door, to find it locked. It was through this door that they had seen the bold detective disappear, and it was in the same direction that the four men proposed to go in search of their daring friend.

The room was in darkness, but Paul soon had the rays of a dark lantern flashing about the place.

"Let us move with caution, " said Harry, taking the lead, and entering the hall through the doorway which Ruggles, in his hasty flight, had left open. Soon voices greeted them from the basement, and a light glimmered through a half-open door at the head of the stairs.

"If we could only put him under down here, " said a voice, which the reader will recognize as that of Nick Brower, the villainous accomplice of Professor Ruggles from the opening of our story.

"Wal, I reckin we kin, " said the villainous companion of Brower. As he spoke, he went to the side of the fallen man-hunter, and placed the point of a knife against his throat.

"What now, pard?

"Dead men tell no tales, Nick. "

"True. Send it home—-"

SPANG!

The sharp report of a revolver wake the echoes once more. The knife dropped from the nerveless grasp of the would-be assassin, and with a howl of pain he began dancing an Irish jig on the stone floor of the cellar.

Nick Brower whirled instantly, snatched a revolver from his hip, to find that four glittering bulldogs confronted him from the stairs.

"Drop that weapon, or we will drop you! " thundered Harry Bernard in a stern voice.

"Trapped! " cried Brower, in a despairing voice.

Then the four men moved down into the cellar and secured Brower and his companion.

"We have made a good haul, " said one of the police officers who accompanied Bernard and Paul, who recognized in Brower an old offender.

Harry Bernard bent quickly and anxiously over the prostrate detective.

"My soul! " uttered the young man, "the villains have killed poor Darrel, I do believe. "

But the young man's belief was unfounded, since some time later Dyke Darrel came to his senses. He was in a bad condition, however, and those who saw him predicted that the detective had followed his last trail. A search of the building brought to light Madge Scarlet, who was fuming angrily over her imprisonment.

"How did this happen? " demanded Bernard, sternly, when he came to question the hag. She was sullen, however, and refused to answer.

"I imagine there is a way to bring your tongue into working order, " said Bernard, in a stern voice.

"I keep a respectable house, sir; you can't harm me. "

"We'll see about that. "

"Did you find any one? " questioned the jezabel in an apparently careless tone.

"We have two of your friends in limbo, " returned Harry. "You will find it no holiday affair to keep a house for the purpose of murder and robbery. Never mind, you need say nothing, for it will not better matters in the least. Come; " and Harry Bernard led the old woman from the cellar.

A patrol wagon bore the prisoners to the lock-up, and Bernard had Dyke Darrel taken to a private hospital, where he could have the best of care. It was some days, however, before the badly battered detective came to his senses sufficiently to converse on the subject of the racket in the building on Clark street.

"My soul! Harry, has nothing been discovered of poor Nell? —was she killed? " questioned the wounded man in a voice wrung with anguish.

"I don't think Nell was mortally hurt, " returned Bernard in a reassuring tone, although he hardly felt hopeful himself. If she was, why should the villains have taken her away, or the villain rather, since, from your account, I judge that but one of them escaped, and he the man with the red hair. "

"Yes, he seemed the chief scoundrel among them. I heard him called Professor Ruggles. "

"He is about as much a professor as I am, " answered Bernard.

"HE is the man we want for that midnight crime on the express train. I have evidence enough now, Dyke, to prove that this man is the guilty principal, and I also believe that one of his accomplices is now in prison. "

"Indeed! "

And then the detective groaned in anguish of spirit and of body. It was hard to lay here, helpless as a child, while the fate of Nell was uncertain, and there was so much need for a keen detective to be afloat. Harry realized how his friend suffered, and soothed him as best he could. "Leave no stone unturned to find her, Harry, " urged the detective. "If you do find and save her, great shall be your reward. If she is dead, then I will see about avenging the deed. "

"And in that you will not be alone, " assured Harry Bernard, a moist light glittering in his eye. Even Dyke Darrel did not suspect how deeply his young friend was interested in the fate of Nell.

The days dragged into weeks ere Dyke Darrel was able to be on his feet again. He was not very strong when he once more took it upon himself to hunt down the scoundrels who had wrecked his happy home. Even the railroad crime was forgotten for the time, so intense was his interest centered in the fate of his sister. If not dead, Dyke Darrel believed she had met with a far worse fate, and it was this thought that nerved him to think of doing desperate work should the cruel abductor ever come before him.

Madge Scarlet was dismissed after an examination, but Nick Brower and his companion were held to await the action of a higher court.

One morning the pallid man in brown suit who had haunted the various depots of the city for several days made a discovery. On one of the early morning trains a man and veiled female had taken passage East.

Dyke Darrel trembled with intense excitement when the depot policeman told him of this.

"Only this morning, you say? "

"It was on one of the earliest trains, I believe, this morning.

"A New York train? "

"I am not sure. I see so many people, you know. You might inquire at the ticket office. "

Dyke Darrel did so.

No ticket for New York had been sold that morning. Then the policeman said that it was possible he might have been mistaken as to the time. It might have been on the previous day he saw the man and his invalid sister.

"Do you know that they took the New York train? " questioned Dyke.

"No; I'm not positive about that, either. You might telegraph ahead and find if such a couple is on the train. "

This was a wise suggestion.

Dyke acted upon it, but failed to derive any satisfaction.

And there was good reason for this, since when leaving Chicago a dark man, with smooth face and gray-tinged hair, accompanied Nell Darrel; whereas, before reaching the borders of New York State, the place of this man had been taken by a man with red beard and hair, blue glasses, and a well-worn silk plug.

This change disturbed identities completely. The change had been made at a way station, without causing remark among the passengers, the most of whom were not through for the great city. Once New York whelmed them, the scheming villain and poor Nell would be lost forever to the man-tracker of the West.

There was a suspicion in the brain of Dyke Darrel that he scarcely dared whisper to his own consciousness. It was that Harper Elliston had a hand in the late villainy. The detective's eyes were open at last, and he realized that his New York friend was not what he seemed. It was this fact that induced Dyke Darrel to believe that the abductor of Nell had turned his face toward the American metropolis. At once he made search for Harry Bernard and Paul Ender.

Neither of them was he able to find, and he had not seen them for two days previous.

It did not matter, however.

Leaving word at the hotel that he had gone to New York, Dyke Darrel once more hastened to the depot, arriving just in time to leap aboard the express headed for the Atlantic seaboard.

The train that had left four hours earlier was almost as fast as the one taken by the detective, so that if no accident happened to the earlier train, there could be little hope of running down his prey before New York was reached.

Nevertheless, Dyke Darrel preserved a hopeful heart, in spite of the terrible anxiety that oppressed him.

The woman who had but a few days before been released from prison was destined to complicate matters and bring about startling and unexpected meetings, as the future will reveal.

When night fell Dyke Darrel found himself yet hundreds of miles from the goal of his hopes and fears.

CHAPTER XXIV.

A RACE FOR LIFE.

As may be supposed, Professor Ruggles was deeply stunned at the coup de main that had deprived him of his fair charge.

Who had robbed him? This was the question that at once suggested itself to his mind, and he found it not difficult to frame an answer, although, until this moment, he had supposed that Madge Scarlet was still in prison.

"It must be her, " he muttered, as he gazed madly at the vacant seat.

"I'm sure it was HER, " said the old man who had first spoken. "A queer, wrinkled old woman, too, she was. "

"Did she say anything? "

"Not a word. "

Mr. Ruggles passed into the next car, hoping to find Nell and the strange old woman there.

He went the whole length of the swift-moving train, only to learn that his fair captive had been spirited away completely.

At first rage consumed the man's senses, and he scarcely realized the dangers of his position.

"I will not give up to such a sneak game, " he muttered at length. "Madge Scarlet has shadowed me for this very purpose, it seems. Can it be possible that the friends of Nell Darrel have employed this hag to rob me of my prize? I will not believe it, for it isn't in the nature of Madge Scarlet to do a good action, not even for pay. No; it is to gratify her own petty scheme of vengeance that she has stolen a march on me; but she will not succeed. I will get on her track and wrest the girl from her hands. "

A minute later Professor Ruggles stood before the conductor.

"When does the next train pass going west? "

"It passes Galien in an hour. "

"Galien? Do you stop there? "

"Yes. "

"Soon? "

"Within five minutes. "

When the train slowed in at the station, Professor Ruggles left the car and entered the depot. Here he would have to wait nearly an hour before the New York train west would pass. It was a tedious wait; but he could do no better. With his hand satchel clutched tightly he paced up and down like a ghost of the night.

He was glad indeed when the train came at length thundering up to the station, He had purchased a ticket for the station from which the abductress had boarded the cars and stolen Nell.

With feverish blood the scheming villain sat by the window and watched the fleeting landscape by the light of the moon. The score of miles that intervened between the station seemed like a hundred to the anxious man who sat and glared at the trees and hills without.

He was in extreme doubt as to his ability to cope with the cunning hag who had ventured so many miles to thwart him, and indulge her own morbid desire for revenge.

At length the whistle sounded announcing the station.

As the train bolted beside another train, bound in the opposite direction, Ruggles glanced into the car not ten feet distant, to make a startling discovery.

He looked squarely into the face of Dyke Darrel, the railroad detective!

Turning his head, the Professor sat quiet. The other train was moving, and Ruggles felt paralyzed at his discovery. Perhaps the detective had not noticed him. He could not understand how the detective had escaped death from the beating he had received in the basement of that building of sin on Clark street.

His own train was moving now, and if he would get off he must be quick about it.

Springing from his seat, he hastened down the aisle.

At the open door he met Dyke Darrel face to face! The recognition was mutual.

The train was moving rapidly out of the station. Soon it would be going at full speed.

Professor Ruggles had two incentives for leaving the train now—one to escape the detective, the other to find Nell and Madge Scarlet.

At first he thought of dashing upon Dyke Darrel and risking all in a swift rush. Second thought, induced by the gleam of a six-shooter in the hand of his enemy, concluded the Professor to seek another course. Turning, he dashed down the length of the car, with Darrel in hot pursuit.

"Halt, or I fire! "

But the detective's cry had no effect.

The half-sleeping passengers were roused by the wonderful movements of the two men.

"Madmen! "

"What IS the trouble? "

Such were the exclamations, as doors slammed, and the two men swept into the next car. From coach to coach sped the pursued and the pursuer. It was a flight for life, on the part of Professor Ruggles.

His plug hat flew off in the chase, and a brakeman who confronted him in the aisle was knocked flat with terrific force.

"Murder! "

And then both men disappeared from the rear platform.

Dyke Darrel believed he had his man in a corner, when he saw him dash through the door at the rear of the long train.

Not so, however.

The desperate Ruggles was ready to do anything rather than come in contact with his relentless foe. He bounded clear of the train, landing in a soft bit of sand, sinking almost to his knees, without harming him in the least.

The detective did not hesitate to follow, but he made a miscalculation, owing to his bodily weakness, and instead of landing on his feet, he came down with stunning force across one of the rails.

Dyke Darrel lay insensible, like one dead.

Had his enemy come upon him then he might have finished the career of the daring man-hunter, without the least danger to himself. For once, Professor Ruggles missed it woefully.

As the detective was ten yards behind the Professor, and the car was going at good speed, there was quite twenty rods difference between the two men when they landed. Dyke Darrel was completely hidden from the sight of Ruggles by a clump of trees.

Ruggles gazed up the track, but saw nothing of his pursuer. He surmised that Dyke Darrel did not leap from the train, but it was likely he would ring the bell and stop the cars at once, so that it would not do to for him to remain in the vicinity unless he wished to collide with the detective.

Another supposition also came to the brain of the villain, preventing his search along the track. If Dyke Darrel had leaped after him, what more natural than his hiding in the clump of timber for the purpose of pouncing upon him when he came up the road.

"I'll not risk it, " muttered Ruggles. "I've other fish to fry just now than looking after detectives. I must find that hag, Madge Scarlet, and get my hands once more on Nell Darrel. "

Then Mr. Ruggles turned his steps in the direction of the station. Already daylight was dawning, and Professor Ruggles was almost beside himself with anxiety. He cursed the woman who had made it necessary for him to leave the train so many miles outside of Gotham. Such a change in the programme might result fatally to himself. Dyke Darrel was hot on the trail now, and it would require the best efforts of a desperate man to throw him off the scent.

The man with the sunset hair was desperate enough. With hurried steps he made his way to the depot. The agent was just shutting up.

"No train, save a way-freight, will be along till night, " he said, in answer to a question from the gentleman with the red locks. Ruggles had taken the precaution to provide himself with a cap from his satchel before presenting himself to the man on duty at the depot.

"One question, " said Ruggles, as the man was about to walk away.

"Well? "

"Did any passengers get off here some hours since from the New York train east? "

"No. "

"Are you sure? "

"None came into the depot, at any rate, " said the man.

"Any passengers get on? "

"Several. "

"Among them an old woman? "

"I saw no woman. "

"You are sure? "

"Of course I am. "

Ruggles was disappointed. Could it be possible that he had been led on a fool's errand after all, and that Madge Scarlet, with her prize, had been concealed on the train, and continued on to New York? The thought was intolerable.

In the meantime, how fared it with Dyke Darrel, who lay stunned and bleeding across the railroad track.

It was almost sun-up before he opened his eyes and groaned. His bed was a hard one, and it seemed as though every bone in his body was broken. The fact was, he was yet sore from his serious fall through the trap into the basement on Clark street, consequently it is little wonder he was badly demoralized, both in mind and body, at his last mishap.

Presently a strange rumbling jar filled his ears. A bend in the road to the west hid the track, but the dazed brain of Dyke Darrel took in the situation nevertheless—a train was thundering down upon him.

A minute more and he would be doomed!

He tried to move—to roll from the track. He could not. His limbs seemed paralyzed. Another second and the train would be upon him!

CHAPTER XXV.

SAVED!

Professor Ruggles had not been remiss in his judgment. It was Madge Scarlet who stole his victim from his arms almost in the hour of his devilish triumph. She did not get on the train from the little way station, however. She was on the train when it drew out of the great city by the lake, but the scheming Ruggles knew it not.

She, too, wore a veil, and was otherwise disguised, and managed not to show herself to the man she had once called friend. Immediately on her release from jail she began to watch Ruggles, who kept himself out of the way, or walked the streets only in disguise.

She haunted the depots of the city, and was lucky enough to see him when he took passage. Quietly boarding the same train, she bided her time, intent on gaining possession of the detective's sister for purposes of her own.

The fires of insanity were already burning in the brain of the convict's wife.

Revenge for past wrongs seemed the sole object of her life now, and this was the incentive that placed her on the track of a fleeing villain and his intended victim.

Madge saw Ruggles when he left the car. She watched her opportunity, and lifting the partially insensible girl, bore her swiftly to the outside, as the train halted for a minute.

She gave vent to a chuckle as the train went thundering on its course.

She had passed from the cars on the opposite side from the depot, and consequently was able to elude the gaze of the depot agent.

Along the track she went, pausing at times to rest, until she was fully a mile from the station. In the shadow of a clump of trees the hag came to a halt and deposited her burden on the ground.

A moan from the drugged and helpless Nell reached her ears.

And then Mrs. Scarlet chuckled the louder.

"Good; she's coming out of her bad spell. I want her to realize her fate, else there wouldn't be the least bit of pleasure in my revenge. "

Removing veil and light cloak, Mrs. Scarlet gazed down into the pallid face of poor Nell, with only hatred gleaming from her sunken, beady eyes.

"Ho! I've outwitted the master devil himself, and now I will have you all to myself, to deal with in a way that will cut to the quick when Dyke Darrel hears of it. "

Nell had on only a light summer robe under the shawl. She looked very innocent and beautiful as she lay there under the gaze of that human hyena.

"Pretty's a picture, " hissed the wicked Madge. "I'll all the more delight in seeing you suffer. Ah! she is coming out of her stupor. How do you feel, dear? "

Nell had opened her eyes and gazed at the wicked face above her, in a dazed semi-consciousness.

No answer was vouchsafed.

Then, in looking about, the gleam of steel lines under the moon's rays seemed to attract the notice of Mrs. Scarlet for the first time — the straight lines that marked the course of the Erie road.

Their glitter seemed to offer a diabolical suggestion to Madge Scarlet.

"Ha! I have it. "

Springing to her feet, she laid her arms about the slender form of the helpless girl, and, lifting her, walked swiftly to the railway track. In the centre, between the rails, she deposited her burden.

"Revenge! sweet revenge! " cackled the hag in a blood-curdling voice.

Again the girl moved and moaned; yet she seemed unable to change her position.

"Rest yourself comfortably, my girl; you won't be in trouble long, " muttered the demon woman, with a grin that was absolutely sickening.

Poor Nell! She lay quite still after that, between the fatal rails, only giving sign of life by a faint moan occasionally.

Mrs. Scarlet retired to her leafy covert to wait the outcome. She could see far beyond the track a farm-house, and near her a heap of ties, and a rude fence—the moonlight revealed everything plainly. Chuckling with hideous satisfaction, the she demon waited the coming of the express that could not be far distant. Morning was already brightening the East.

Far away was the sound of a moving train. The sullen, distant roar sent a thrill to the heart of the demon woman, who crouched in the bushes to await the completion of her unhallowed revenge.

The sullen jar seemed to act like a shock of electricity on the nerves of Nell Darrel. She felt a strange and awful numbness. With a mighty effort the girl roused herself to a consciousness of her awful position.

Louder and louder roared the train. It was but a mile distant now, and the road was straight.

Nell raised her head, and resting on her hands gazed down the track where, in the distance, gleamed the light of the locomotive.

"God help me! " moaned the poor girl. Then she tried to throw herself from the track, but she could not. Her limbs were numb, and refused to obey her will.

A wild laugh rang out on the moonlit air.

Madge Scarlet sprang up and glared through the bushes at her victim with maniacal delight.

"Ha' ha! You cannot escape! Them pretty limbs'll be crushed and torn asunder! the white flesh cut and gashed, and that delicate body made a horrid mass of blood and mangled fragments! THEN I will present them to you, Dyke Darrel. Ho! ho! "

Her voice was raised to a high pitch now, and even reached the ears of the startled Nell.

No help, no hope!

On thundered the iron monster.

On and on till the eye of the engineer catches sight of something on the track—SOMETHING!

Quickly the engine is reversed and the air brakes come into play.

Too late!

A moan of agonized terror falls from the lips of the half dead girl, and then she sank helplessly to the ground. At the same instant help came from an unexpected source.

A man dashed swiftly through the moonlight and flung a heavy oak tie in front of the slackened engine.

A rumble and a jar, and then the train came to a dead stop, within three feet of the prostrate girl!

It was a narrow escape.

The man who had come so unexpectedly out of the shadows dragged Nell from her dangerous position. The engineer and fireman came down and congratulated the young man on his presence.

"The brakes couldn't quite do it, " said the engineer. "That tie saved the girl, with no damage to the train. "

"It seems to be a lucky accident all round, " said the young man, who had laid Nell on a safe spot, and now turned his attention to assisting in removing the obstruction from the rails.

"Yes. Who is she? "

"I can't say. "

"Well, I must be on the way, " uttered the engineer, "we are behind time now. "

By this time the conductor was on the ground, but the train was running again, and he received a full explanation from the engineer afterward.

When the young man made a closer inspection of the girl he had rescued, a cry of surprise fell from his lips.

"As I live, it is Nell Darrel! "

But she could not speak to thank him for his act, since she had fainted.

Lifting ner tenderly the young man turned his steps in the direction of the farm-house, where he had been stopping during the past two days.

"Curse you! curse you! " were the venomous words flung after the man by Madge Scarlet.

But she dared not interfere to prevent the rescue.

When Nell Darrel again opened her eyes, it was to find herself calmly resting on a couch in a little room, whose cozy appearance was like home indeed. And the face that bent over her was not that of a stranger. Could it be that she was dreaming?

"Thank Heaven! " murmured a manly voice, and then a mustached lip bent and pressed a clinging kiss to the cheek of poor Nell.

"Harry, dear Harry! "

Thus had the lovers met after many long months of separation.

A smile rested on the face of the fair girl as she held Harry's hand while he talked of the past.

She explained as best she could the strangeness of her situation; but everything was so much like a dream, it was a hard matter to reconcile some of the events of the past few weeks.

"The end draws nigh, " assured young Bernard, after a time. "If the notorious man calling himself Ruggles was on the train, he will, on discovering his loss, turn back, and then I will capture him. "

CHAPTER XXVI.

THE MYSTERIOUS WART.

We left Dyke Darrel, the detective, in a critical position on the railroad track, with the roar of a freight engine in his ears. The rays of the rising sun touched the glittering rails as the long train swept around the bend upon doomed Dyke Darrel.

One more tremendous effort on the part of the detective, and he succeeded in throwing his body squarely across one of the rails. In this position he hung a helpless weight, with the hoarse roar of the engine making anything but sweet music to his fainting soul.

Ha! Look! A hand is outstretched to save at the last moment, and Dyke Darrel is jerked from under the smoking wheels, even as their breath fans his fevered cheek.

The train swept on.

A cheer greeted the man who had come opportunely to the rescue as the engine swept on its course.

And a little later a man, young, yet whose boyish face bore marks of dissipation, stood beside the detective and gazed into his face now for the first time.

"Great Caesar! "

The young man started as though cut by a knife, and bent low over the fallen detective, who was now struggling to a sitting posture.

When he looked into the face of his rescuer he uttered a great cry.

"My soul! how came you here, Martin Skidway? "

"I am a fugitive, " answered the young convict. "It wasn't through your good will that I got out of prison, I can tell you that. Had I known who it was on the track, I might not have put out my hand to save. "

The detective regarded the speaker in no little amazement. This was the second time he had escaped from the Missouri prison, which argued well for the man's keenness and capability, or else ill for the official management of the prison.

"It was from the St. Louis prison that I escaped, " explained Martin Skidway a little later. "I never got inside the State institution a second time. I've had a sweet time of it thus far. "

"Tell me how you made your escape, " said Dyke Darrel, who sat with his back against a tree, and regarded the young counterfeiter in wonder.

"There isn't much to tell, " returned Skidway. "I had no assistance, but it seems that a pair of burglars had broken out by filing off the grating to one of the corridor windows, and the opening had not been repaired when I was taken to the jail. I was left in the corridor a minute while the jailor was attending some other prisoners, and that minute gave me the opportunity. I mounted a chair, climbed through the window, and made my escape by the light of the moon. Of course there was a big search, but I remained hidden in an old cellar under a deserted house in a grove within the city limits, for several days, and finally made good my escape from the State. "

"And now? "

"I am going to put the ocean between me and the beaks of American law. "

Dyke Darrel regarded the speaker with mingled emotions. He saw in this daring young fellow much talent, that had it been rightly directed, might have made an honorable place in the world for Martin Skidway.

"I am helpless to arrest your steps just at present, " groaned the detective. "Would you do it after what has happened, if you were in a condition to do so? " demanded the convict, bending over the man on the ground, regarding him with a menacing look.

"Duty often calls one to do that which is disagreeable, " answered Dyke Darrel. A deep frown mantled the brows of the convict.

"I see that my mercy was misdirected, " he said. "It seems that I have saved your life only to give you a chance to dog me to doom. Think you I am fool enough to permit this? "

There was a menace in the man's voice that Dyke Darrel did not like.

"I am at present helpless, " he said. "I don't imagine you will harm a man who is in no condition to injure you if he would. "

"But you can talk. The first man who comes along will hear from you that an escaped convict is in the rural districts of New York, and a telegram will set ten thousand officers on the lookout for me. Without such information I would not be recognized in this community. I am a desperate man, Dyke Darrel, and do not propose to sacrifice myself for your benefit. "

"What will you do? "

"One of two things. "

"Well? "

"You must solemnly swear that you will never reveal to another that I am in this region, and swear also to make no effort to capture me under a month, or else I shall have a painful duty to perform. "

"Go on! "

"Will you take the required oath? '

"Certainly not. "

"Then the other alternative is alone left me, Dyke Darrel. "

"And that? "

"DEATH TO YOU! "

Straightening to his full height after uttering the three terrible words, Martin Skidway snatched a heavy iron bolt from the ground, that had lain long beside the track, and raised it above the head of helpless Dyke Darrel.

"Martin Skidway, hold! "

The words of the detective came forth in a thrilling cry.

An instant the would be assassin stayed his hand.

"You agree to my terms? "

"No; but—"

"Then you must die. It will be considered an accident, and no one will suspect my hand in the affair. "

Again the young convict poised his weapon for deadly work. On the instant the rumble of wheels met the ears of Martin Skidway.

A wagon containing two men was in sight, moving down a road that ran parallel with the railway at this point. It was evident that the occupants of the vehicle had seen Skidway, and to strike now would but add to the vengeance of pursuit and punishment. With a curse, he dropped the iron bolt and turned to flee.

"Dyke Darrel, if you inform on me, I will kill you at another time! " hissed the convict.

Then he rushed from the spot and disappeared.

As the wagon came opposite it halted, and the cries of Dyke Darrel brought both men to his side.

"Hello! is this you? " cried a cheery voice, and the next instant Dyke Darrel was lifted to his feet by the strong hand of Harry Bernard.

It was a happy and unexpected meeting. Harry had good news to tell, and when Dyke Darrel, assisted by his friend, reached the farmhouse where Nell had found safety and shelter, the detective was strong enough to stand, and assist himself in no small degree.

Mutual explanations were entered into, and, as may be supposed, the meeting between brother and sister was a happy one indeed. Harry was the hero of the hour.

When Dyke Darrel spoke of Martin Skidway, and the part he had acted in saving his life, a word of admiration fell from the lips of Nell.

But when Dyke proceeded to the conclusion, the girl's face blanched, and she had no word of commendation left for the miserable convict, who, after all, possessed but little honor.

"So Aunt Scarlet is in the neighborhood; and also your abductor, " mused the detective. "The trail is becoming hot, indeed. "

"It is, for a fact, " admitted Harry. "I believe, if the truth was known, this man Ruggles will prove to be the man we want. Have you that handkerchief with you, Dyke, that we found in the coat of the rascal who attempted your murder in St. Louis? "

This was several hours after the events of the morning, and Nell was now resting in a large wooden rocker, very weak, yet feeling remarkably well, considering the siege she had passed through during the past two weeks and more. Dyke Darrel and Harry were the only occupants of the room, the farmer being at his work in the field, and his good wife attending preparations for supper in the kitchen.

"I have kept the tell-tale handkerchief through it all, " answered the detective, at the same time producing the article from a receptacle beneath, his shirt.

"It's a wonder this was not discovered when you were in the hands of the thugs of Chicago. "

"I wasn't closely searched, I suppose. You and the boys were too close after them. "

"You give me too much credit, Dyke, " returned Harry Bernard, modestly. "I've a question to ask. "

"Ask as many as you like. "

"Was it the fact of my hand fitting this bloody imprint that so startled you in the St. Louis hotel? "

"Did I not so claim at the time? "

"Perhaps; but wasn't there another coincidence that gave you reason to suspect me?

"There might have been. "

"I thought so. It was the imprint of a large wart, such as this on the handkerchief, that made you look with suspicion upon me. Is it not so? "

Harry held up his hand, so that a wart on the little finger was plainly revealed, and which, when he placed his hand against the tell- tale handkerchief, fitted the marks perfectly.

"Forgive me, Harry, " cried the detective, quickly. "I know now that it was only a remarkable duplicate; the wart belonged to another hand than yours. The print of the wart was also on the bosom of Arnold Nicholson's white shirt bosom, where a bloody hand had fallen. I made this discovery when I examined the body of my dead friend. Circumstantial evidence pointed to you, and yet I doubted —"

"I understand, " interrupted Harry. "My hand is indeed a duplicate of the assassin's. It is a wonder that I have not been arrested ere this by some of the detectives who are engaged in working up this case. "

"Why so? "

"Because you are not the only one who made the discovery of the wart that adorned the hand of the assassin. A reporter got hold of the story and published it. Don't you remember? "

"I haven't read the papers closely since the murder. "

"But I have, and so has the man who killed Nicholson. "

"Indeed? "

"He soon learned that officers of the law were all looking for a man with a large wart on the second joint of the little finger of the right hand. This fact made him nervous, and one night he severed the wart, and flung it from him, since which time he has breathed easier."

A low exclamation from the lips of Nell startled both men.

155

CHAPTER XXVII.

THE STORY OF A WART.

"Nell, what is it? " questioned the surprised detective.

Harry regarded the girl with a queer smile. Perhaps he knew what had brought the exclamation to the lips of Miss Darrel.

"I know a man who has lost a wart, " she said, slowly, a deepening pallor coming to her cheeks.

"His name? " questioned Dyke Darrel, eagerly.

But the girl did not immediately answer. It seemed that something moved her deeply.

"Was it Professor Ruggles? " questioned Harry, in order to help the young girl out.

"No, " she said.

"Who then? "

"Harper Elliston! "

A grave look chased the smile from the face of Harry Bernard.

The girl's announcement seemed to prove a revelation to him, even as it did to Dyke Darrel.

"I did not know the man who severed the wart from his hand, " said Harry Bernard, after a brief silence, "but suspected that it was Darlington Ruggles. It seems now that I was correct. "

"How is that? "

"Have you not guessed the truth, " queried Harry Bernard. "I made the discovery some time since that the red-haired man and Harper Elliston were one and the same. "

This came as a revelation to both the detective and his sister.

"I have had suspicions, " said Dyke Darrel, "but never anything definite regarding the villainy of this man Elliston. He has played his cards well, but I became undeceived not long after this great railroad crime. That he was not my friend I discovered, and then I resolved to watch him. I have reason to believe that it was to him I owe my arrest in Burlington, Iowa. I now see the truth, that under the assumed name of Hubert Vander, Elliston ruined a young girl of Burlington, and, it may be, murdered her father, wealthy Captain Osborne. It would be strange indeed, should the trail that ends with the capture of the express robber also bring to punishment the assassin of the Burlington Captain. "

"It seems likely to end in that way, " returned Harry.

"Let us hear what Nell has to say with regard to the wart, " said the detective, turning to his sister.

"It will require but a few words to do that, " said Nell Darrel. "I always noticed a peculiarly shaped wart on the finger of Mr. Elliston's shapely right hand, and once he remarked upon it to me, saying that it was a disfigurement, and that he meant to have it removed sometime. I think it was the first time I met Mr. Elliston after the terrible news of the mid night express tragedy that I noticed the absence of the wart, and a bit of surgeon's plaster covering the spot. I laughed over his having undergone such a severe surgical operation, and he seemed to take it in good part, assuring me that HE was the surgeon who amputated the excrescence with a razor. Of course I thought nothing strange of it at the time. "

"You said the wart had a peculiar shape? How is that? " questioned Harry Bernard.

"It was large, and was composed of two crowns. I think, perhaps two warts had grown together at the roots. "

"Exactly. Would you know the wart if you should see it again? "

"I think I should. "

"So would I, " cried the detective.

Then Harry Bernard drew a small vial from his pocket and held it up to view. A small object, submerged in alcohol, was visible. When placed in the hand of Nell, the girl at once exclaimed:

"That is certainly the wart that once disfigured the hand of Harper Elliston! "

"Where did you get it? " questioned Dyke Darrel, now deeply interested at the links that were being rapidly forged in the chain of evidence.

"Dyke, you know that when I left Woodburg some months ago, I went from among you under a cloud? "

"I will not dispute you—"

"No explanation is necessary on your part, Dyke. I imagine I was as much to blame as anybody. Nell and I quarreled, and I imagined that the handsome, elderly New Yorker had stepped into my shoes, so far as she was concerned. I did not like the man, and so I resolved to investigate for myself, and if I found that he was not worthy of Nell, whom I loved and should always love while life lasted, I determined to expose him, and save your sister. During the past few months I have been making this investigation, to find that the supposed immaculate Harper Elliston is known in Gotham in certain circles as a gambler and villain of the deepest dye. He has committed some crimes that are worse than murder. Now, as to the wart: It was soon after I had heard of the murder on the express train, that while riding in the smoking car of an emigrant train in Iowa, I saw an old man deliberately slice a huge wart from his little finger with a keen-edged knife. The wart fell under the seat and rolled at my feet. The old man made no effort to recover it, but wrapped his bleeding hand in a handkerchief and muttered: 'THAT witness will never come up to trouble me. ' There was something in the man's voice that sounded familiar, and the strange whiteness of his hands aroused my suspicions, for in dress and appearance the man was a laborer of the lower class. Curiosity, if nothing stronger, prompted me to take possession of the severed wart that had rolled at my feet. Soon after that I read the notice in a newspaper, to the effect that the assassin of the express train had left the imprint of a wart on the bosom of the dead man's shirt. Since that time I have regarded hands with no little interest, and have looked for the old man of the emigrant car in vain. "

"An interesting recital, " said the detective, when Harry Bernard came to a pause. "Knowing all this, you kept it from me at St. Louis."

"My reason for that was, that I did not care to arouse any foolish theories. Of course, the reporter's story might have been false. The wart on my own hand, somewhat similar to this, led me to keep my own council as a matter of personal safety. Although I suspected Elliston, I had no proof, since I had forgotten the fact of his ever having a wart on the little finger of his right hand. My principal hope has been in finding the old man of the emigrant train. "

"You have not found him? "

"Not unless Elliston is the man. "

"Did you suspect this before now? "

"I did; now I am convinced. "

Just then Harry Bernard chanced to raise his eyes and gaze out of the open window.

He came suddenly to his feet with a startled exclamation.

Dyke Darrel glanced out of the window to notice a bent old man, with white hair and beard, moving away from the vicinity of the house. Evidently he had been looking into the room, if not listening to the conversation of the trio.

"Saints of Rome! there is the old man of the emigrant train now! "

Dyke Darrel staggered to the window, while Harry Bernard rushed swiftly from the farm-house.

CHAPTER XXVIII.

THE REVELATIONS OF A SATCHEL.

"Hello, old man! "

"Eh? "

The man stopped, stared at Harry Bernard as if puzzled, and then began to grin.

"I want to speak with you, sir. "

"Sortin, sortin you can. "

"Who are you? "

"Sam Wiggs o' Yonkers. Wat can I do for ye, mister? "

The old fellow seemed honest enough, and as Harry glanced at the dirty hands, he saw nothing to excite his suspicions.

"Are you a relative of Mr. —-? " naming the farmer who owned the place on which they stood.

"Wal, not as I knows on, " drawled the old fellow, laughing until his old head seemed ready to topple from his shoulders. "No blood relation, any how, sir. You see, my wife's cousin's aunt's husband's brother Jerry was a cousin to Nicodemus Dunce, who, if I don't disremember, was related in some way to Isacker Pete's wife's sister, and she was this ere man's niece, or somethin' o' that sort, but we ain't blood related nohow. "

"I should think not, " answered Harry, and then he returned to the house, while the old man Wiggs proceeded unmolested on his way.

"At a first glance, he DID resemble the man of the emigrant train strongly, " muttered Bernard, "but I see now that I was mistaken. "

"Well, how did you make out, Harry? "

"This was from Dyke Darrel, who had been watching proceedings from the window.

"A case of mistaken identity, " answered the young man, with a laugh. "I was sure I had found the right man when I saw that old chap crossing the yard, but it seems that I was mistaken. "

"Are you sure of it? "

"I suppose I am. "

Dyke Darrel watched the retreating form of the old man with no little curiosity, however, until his bent form was lost to view down the winding road. Naturally suspicious, the detective more than half believed that the seemingly aged man had not come to the farm-house for any good purpose.

"I can't help thinking that Wiggs, as he called himself, is destined to give us trouble, Harry, " the detective said, at length.

"An inoffensive old man, " asserted Bernard. At the same time, however, he was not fully content to let the matter rest as it was.

"It might be well enough to watch the old fellow, at any rate, " said Dyke Barrel, rising and walking twice across the room, peering nervously out of the window in the direction in which old Wiggs had gone.

"Keep quiet, Dyke, " said Bernard. "I will shadow the old fellow, and see if he is other than he seems. "

Bernard was on the point of leaving the room, when a youth appeared, walking swiftly toward the farm-house from the direction of the station. One glance sufficed to show both men the genial face of the boy Paul Ender.

"So you have Paul with you, Harry? " said the detective with a pleased smile.

"He is my shadow, and I have found him true and brave, " answered Harry, at the same time glancing toward Nell, who had told him of the lad's defense of her against the villain Elliston.

"I can testify to his bravery, " said the girl. "Paul and I are great friends. "

A minute later, young Ender entered the presence of the trio, and deposited a black satchel in the middle of the floor.

"I have committed a theft, " said the boy, with a queer look on his face, "and am here to throw myself on the mercy of the court. "

"You speak in riddles, " said Bernard. "I've been on a bully lay, as the peelers say, and I believe have made a discovery, although it may amount to nothing after all. "

"Go on. "

"I've seen the man with the red hair and beard. "

"When? "

"Where? "

"Over by the depot. I saw him go into an old out-house with this satchel in his hand. "

"Indeed! "

"Go on. "

"I was on the watch, and when he came out I saw, not Brother Ruggles, but a lean old man, with white locks and beard, who seemed to walk with great difficulty. "

"Ah! "

"Indeed! "

"He hobbled away, and failed to take the satchel with him. At first I could not believe that the sorrel gent and the old chap were the same. I learned this by investigation. When, after waiting a spell, and no sunset-haired gent came forth, I proceeded to investigate, and found this satchel, which, under the law of military necessity, I proceeded to confiscate, that the ends of justice might be furthered. If

I have done wrong, I am ready to throw myself on the mercy of the court, and be forgiven. "

"You have done right, " cried Dyke Barrel. "Have you opened the satchel? "

"No. It is locked, and I haven't a key that will fit. "

Harry Bernard produced several keys, none of which fitted the lock to the satchel.

"What are we to do? " cried Bernard. The satchel is securely locked, and its owner has the key. "

"This is no time for ceremony or undue squeamishness! " uttered Dyke Darrel. "We are on the eve of an important discovery, and I propose to make no delays. "

Then, drawing a knife from his pocket, the detective bent over the satchel and slit the sides at one stroke. "

"That will open it if a key won't, " he remarked, with grim satisfaction.

The contents of the satchel were a revelation.

Red wigs and a complete suit of clothes, besides paints and powders.

Harry uttered an exclamation.

"Just as I suspected, " uttered Dyke Darrel. "You made no, mistake when you suspected that old man who just now left this vicinity. Doubtless he forgot his satchel, or else thought it safe until his return. Paul, my boy, you have done a good thing, and shall be promoted. We must now make it a point to intercept old Wiggs. "

"Doubtless he has gone to the depot. "

"How far is that from here? "

"Two miles. "

"When does the train pass? " questioned Dyke Darrel.

"I cannot say. "

"Nor I. "

"Ask the farmer's wife. "

Paul sped from the room.

"The New York express goes in ten minutes, " said the boy, on his return.

"In ten minutes? Then we have no time to lose, " cried Dyke, turning to the door.

"Dyke, what would you do? " demanded Nell at this moment.

"Capture your enemy and mine—-"

"But you are not strong enough to take the trail. Stay with me. "

He interrupted her with:

"Nell, I never felt stronger in my life. I mean to put the bracelets on the villain's wrists with my own hands. "

"Dyke, leave it to me, " urged Harry Bernard.

But the detective's blood was up, and he would listen to no one. He was determined to be in at the death, and for the time his old strength seemed coursing in his veins. He hastened from the house, and ascertaining that a horse was in the barn, he at once sprang to the animal's back.

"You are unarmed? " said Bernard. "Yes, but—"

"Take this; I will quickly follow, " and the young man thrust a revolver into the hand of Dyke Darrel. "Do nothing rash until help arrives, Dyke. Our game is desperate, and will fight hard if cornered."

"I am aware of that, but I do not fear him. Ha! what is that? "

"The roar of the train. "

"Then time is short. "

The horse and rider shot away down the country road like an arrow, or a bird. On and on, with the speed of the wind, and yet the lightning express made even greater speed than did the detective's horse.

With a roar and a rush the train swept past.

Too late!

Dyke Darrel drew rein at the depot just as the train swept madly away on its course to the great city, and on the rear platform stood the old man who had peered into the farm-house window but a short time before.

It was an aggravating situation.

"You can use the telegraph, " suggested the depot agent, when Darrel unbosomed himself to him.

"Quick! Send word to the next station, and have the man detained. "

The ticket agent went to his instrument and ticked off the desired information.

A little later came the reply:

"No such person on the train. "

A malediction fell from the detective's lips. Was his enemy to thus outwit him always?

CHAPTER XXIX.

RETRIBUTION.

A tall, handsome man of middle-age stood picking his teeth with a jaunty air beside the desk of a down-town boarding-house, when his occupation, if such we may call it, was interrupted by a touch on his arm.

Looking down, the gentleman saw a small, ragged urchin standing near.

"It is yourn—10 cents, please. "

The boy held out a yellow envelope, on which was scrawled the name "Harper Elliston. "

The gentleman dropped the required bit of silver into the boy's hand with the air of a king, and then tore open the envelope.

"MR. ELLISTON: Meet me at Room 14, Number 388 Blank street, at seven this evening, SHARP. Business of importance.

"B. "

The contents of the envelope puzzled Mr. Elliston, who had been but ten days in New York since his return from the West. He had several acquaintances whose names might with appropriateness be signed B. "I don't think there'll be any harm in meeting Mr. B. at the place mentioned. It may be of importance, as he says. If it should be a trap set by Dyke Darrel—but, pshaw! that man is dead. I had it from the lips of Martin Skidway, and he knew whereof he spoke. I will call at 388, let the consequences be what they may. " Thus decided a cunning villain, and in so doing went to his own doom.

Ten days had Dyke Darrel and his friend Bernard searched the city of New York ere they found their prey. Once found, the detective resolved upon a novel manner of procedure for his capture. The sending of the letter was part of the scheme. Had this failed, then a bolder move would have been made.

But it did not fail.

When Mr. Elliston rapped at room 14, number 388 Blank street, the door was opened, admitting the visitor to a small room containing a bed, a few necessary articles of furniture, and a curtained alcove.

The door was suddenly closed and locked behind Elliston, light was turned on fully, and then the visitor found himself confronted by Harry Bernard, whom he had met once or twice in Woodburg, many months before.

"Eh! " ejaculated Elliston. "So you are the man who wrote that note requesting an interview? Well, I am glad to see you, Mr. Bernard, " and Elliston held out his hand, with a smile wreathing his thin lips.

"I imagined you would be, " returned the youth. "I am glad to see you so well. Fact is, you are badly wanted out in Illinois at the present time. "

"I am sorry that I cannot accommodate my friends out there, " returned Elliston, with a frown; "but it is wholly out of the question. I think I will bid you good evening, Mr. Bernard. I cannot waste precious time here. "

He turned and grasped the door-knob. It did not yield to his touch.

"Not just yet, Mr. Elliston, " said Harry. "I wish to ask you a few questions. "

"Well? "

"What do you know of the murder of Arnold Nicholson on the midnight express, south of Chicago, some weeks ago? "

"I read of it, of course. "

Mr. Elliston pulled nervously at his glove as he answered.

"What do you know of the disappearance of Captain Osborne and the death of his daughter? " persisted Bernard.

"Do you suppose I have nothing to do but answer such nonsensical questions? " demanded Elliston, angrily. "Open this door and let me pass out. "

"Not yet. I wish to tell you a little story, Mr. Elliston. "

"I haven't time to listen. "

"Nevertheless, you must take the time, " said Harry Bernard, sternly. "Don't attempt to make trouble, sir; you will get the worst of it if you do. "

There was a glitter in the eyes of the speaker that was not pleasant to see.

Mr. Elliston sank to a chair, and with an air of resignation said:

"Well, well, this is impudent, but I will listen if it will gratify you. "

"It certainly will. I wish to start out with the assertion that you DO know something about the crime on the midnight express, and I will try and convince you that *I* know what part you acted in the murder of one of the best men in the service of the express company. Don't lose your temper, sir, but listen? "

"I am listening. "

There was a sullen echo in the man's voice that boded an outburst soon.

"A gentleman of your build and complexion boarded the train at a station just south of Chicago one night in April. At another station two companions joined this man, according to previous agreement. One was almost a boy in years, an escaped convict; and these three men during the night entered the express car, murdered the agent, and went through the safe. Just before reaching Black Hollow the three men left the car. One of the three was tall and had red hair and beard. This man, after the slaughter, left a trace behind that has led to his identity. He left the imprint of a bloody hand on a white handkerchief that he took from the pocket of his victim. That handkerchief was afterward found, and the bloody mark compared with the hand of the assassin. "

"That could hardly be possible. Hands are many of them alike, " articulated Mr. Elliston, nervously.

"True, but in this case a wart, of peculiar shape, gave the man away. The mark of his bloody hand, leaving the wart's impress, was not only on the handkerchief, but left against the white shirt-front of the murdered man as well. The man who committed the murder read of the clew in a Chicago paper, and, to obliterate the tell-tale evidence, he cut the wart from his hand and dropped it under the seat while journeying through Iowa in disguise, on an emigrant train. "

The face of Elliston had become white as death, and he trembled from head to foot. If Bernard had doubted before, he doubted now no longer.

"A nice story, " finally sneered Bernard's visitor. "When did you learn so much? "

"Weeks ago—"

"And you have permitted this villain to run at large so long! "

"Well, I propose to see that he does not flaunt his crimes in the face of the world longer. "

Then, with a quick movement, the youth drew a vial from his pocket and held it up to view, exhibiting to the dilating eyes of the New Yorker a large wart with a double top.

"Just remove the glove from your right hand, Mr. Elliston. I think we will find a scar there that this wart will fit—"

"Furies! this is too much, " cried Elliston, coming to his feet, white with rage and fear.

"Stop. Keep your temper, " warned Bernard. "I wish to bring a witness; one that has been your companion in crime. "

The curtain over the alcove was brushed aside, and a man stepped forth, a man with red whiskers and hair, the latter surmounted with a glossy plug hat.

Elliston stared like one bereft of sense and life.

"Allow me to introduce Professor Darlington Ruggles, Mr. Elliston, " uttered Harry Bernard in a mocking voice.

"Hades! what does this mean? " and the trapped villain staggered, clutching the back of a chair for support.

"It means that your race of crime and diabolism is run, Harper Elliston! "

Red hair and beard were suddenly swept aside, a revolver was thrust into the startled countenance of Elliston; he looked, and could only utter:

"DYKE DARREL, THE DETECTIVE! "

"Do you deny your guilt, scoundrel? "

But Harper Elliston sank to a seat, and bowed his head, while drops of cold sweat covered his forehead.

The touch of cold steel and click of closing bracelets roused him.

He was helpless now, for his wrists were encircled by handcuffs. Black despair confronted the villain.

Dyke Darrel went through the pockets of his prisoner and found a revolver, an ugly looking clasp knife, and other articles of a nature that served to show that the owner was not pursuing an honest calling.

"Do you remember that night on the dock beside the river, Elliston? " questioned Bernard, bending suddenly over the prisoner.

But no answer came from the bloodless lips of the cornered villain.

"It was I who tore your mask of red hair from your head that night. I had mistrusted you for a villain, and I meant to unmask you to save Nell Darrel, whom I loved, from your wiles. You struck me with a knife and pushed me into the river. I, however, was not harmed. The point of your knife glanced on a small book that I carried in an inner pocket. I escaped from the river, and resolved to follow you to your doom. I overheard your plans of abducting Nell Darrel, when you fired at my masked face that night as I peered into Mother Scarlet's room. I then knew you to be a villain of the deepest dye. Since, I learned that you were the man in disguise on the emigrant train in

Iowa, and this wart will, with other evidence, condemn you before an honest jury of your peers. "

A groan alone answered the denouement made by Harry Bernard.

Dyke Darrel removed the glove from his prisoner's right hand, and exposed a scarcely-healed scar near the joint of the little finger. The chain of evidence was complete. The red hair in the clutches of the murdered Nicholson had evidently been torn from the false beard of the disguised assassin.

The New Yorker was removed from the house and taken at once to prison. From thence, on the following morning, Dyke Darrel set out on his return to the Garden City with Elliston in charge.

Harry Bernard remained over at the farm-house in New York State to see Nell, who had been left in the care of Paul Ender. Nell had almost entirely recovered from the shock of her recent treatment, and was overjoyed at the outcome of her friends' visit to New York.

"Elliston will be convicted and hanged, " was Bernard's verdict.

On the very day of Harry's arrival at the farm-house, he, with the old farmer, was summoned to visit one who had met with a fatal accident and was about to die.

It proved to be Martin Skidway, who lay on a barn floor with his head in his mother's lap, gasping his life away, an ugly wound in his side.

He had accidentally shot himself and was rapidly sinking. A fugitive in hiding for weeks, his life had been an intolerable one. Now that he was dying, he made a full confession, admitting his own hand in the awful railroad crime, and implicating two others, Elliston and Nick Brower. Sam Swart had been one of them, but he was known to be dead.

"Without HIS urging I would never have stained my hands; in fact, it was Elliston who struck the blow that killed the express messenger. "

Without this confession, there was evidence enough to convict the New Yorker; with it, both Brower and the principal were found guilty of murder in the first degree and sentenced to the gallows. Nick Brower was the only one of the four who expiated his crime on the gallows. Harper Elliston died in prison by his own hand.

He left a note admitting the express crime, and also confessing to the murder of Captain Osborne and the ruin of his daughter Sibyl. His was a fitting end to a career of unparalleled crime.

****

We now draw a veil over the scene.

Harry Bernard and Nell Darrel were, soon after the arrest and death of Elliston, happily married.

Dyke Darrel considers the events leading up to the capture and punishment of those engaged in the crime of the midnight express as among the most thrilling and wonderful of his detective experience. To Harry Bernard and Paul Ender he gives a large share of the credit, and with them shared the reward. Bernard has of late worked in conjunction with Dyke Darrel on other cases, and is fast winning a reputation second only to that of the great railroad detective himself.

THE END.

WON BY CRIME

CHAPTER I

A young girl, about eighteen, with a slender, elegant form, beautiful straight features, and eyes of softest darkness, sitting before a large table covered with maps and drawings, which she was trying vainly to study.

"It is no use! " she cried, at last, pushing back the mass of thick black hair falling over her white brow; "I shall never be able to get India by heart, unless I can see the places. I wish papa would let us go reconnoitering amongst the ruined temples and other mysterious buildings; it is so annoying staying here day after day, never seeing anything outside the palace'

"My dear Lianor, " said her companion, a young man scarcely older than herself, and wonderfully like her, "what new idea, have you got now? "

"An idea of seeing more of the curious places I have read so much about. Fancy living a lifetime in a country and never going beyond one town! If I do not get some excitement, I shall die of ennui, so I warn you. "

"I quite agree with you, and if uncle would only let us, it would be delightful, seeking out the temples so long deserted. But you know he would not, " shrugging his shoulders.

"I'm not so sure of that. Papa never refuses me anything, and when he sees it is necessary to my happiness I should go, he will consent. Anyhow, I will try, " jumping eagerly to her feet. "Come, Leone"

Her cousin rose, and took the white, outstretched hand; then like two children they crossed the beautiful marble hall, until, arriving before a door draped with rich curtains, Lianor paused and softly knocked.

"Come in! " rather impatiently.

With a smile Lianor opened the door, and entered, followed by Pantaleone.

In the room, handsomely fitted up as a study, sat a fine-looking, middle-aged man, busily wilting; his dark face wore an expression of severity as he glanced toward the intruders.

It quickly faded, however, on seeing the pretty figure standing there; instead, a gentle smile wreathed his lips.

"Well, Lianor, dearest, what is it? "

"Papa, " and the girl stole noiselessly behind his chair, winding her arms around his neck. "I am so miserable, I have nothing to amuse me, and unless you do something to make me happier, I shall go melancholy mad! "

"My dearest child, what is the matter? Are you ill? " anxiously turning to peer into the lovely face.

"No, papa; but I am so tired of this life. "

"That is not like my little girl. And I have tried hard to make you happy. Nothing in reason have I refused you—jewels, such as a queen might envy; priceless stuffs to deck your pretty form, and other things which no girl of your age ever possessed, " reproachfully.

Lianor bent down, and kissed his brow, lovingly—repentingly.

"You have been a great deal too good to me. But there is something more I wish to ask; it will make me happy if you will grant my request. "

"We shall see. Tell me first what it is. "

Lianor briefly related her wish to visit the old temple which lay beyond Goa, to search with Panteleone the curious old ruins she had so often read of in her studies.

Don Gracia looked grave; evidently this project did not find much favor in his eyes.

A Portuguese by birth, but sent to Goa as Viceroy, Don Garcia de Sa had lived there long enough to know the treacherous natures of the

Brahmins who dwelt near, and feared to let his child run the risk of being found and captured.

But as Lianor had truly remarked, he loved his daughter so passionately that he very rarely refused her anything, even though he doubted the wisdom of complying with her wishes.

"Papa"—the sweet voice was very coaxing, and the red lips close to his cheek—"say yes, darling; it will make me so happy. "

"But suppose any danger should threaten you? "

"I should be there to defend my cousin with my life! " Leone cried, fervently.

Don Gracia smiled.

"You speak bravely, my boy; but as yet you are very young. However, as Lianor has set her heart upon this expedition, I suppose I must say yes. In case of danger, I will send some soldiers to escort you. "

"Oh, thank you, papa! I am so glad! Come, Leone, we will make haste, so as to set off ere the day gets more advanced. "

And warmly embracing her father, the girl sped swiftly away, followed by her cousin.

In half an hour the cortege was ready, and, after some little hesitation on Don Garcia's part, they started.

Lianor, with her two favorite maids, Lalli and Tolla, were cosily seated in a palanquin carried by four strong men. Before, clearing her path from all difficulties, went a body of twenty-five soldiers. Beside her, Panteleone kept up a cheerful conversation, pointing out the beauties of the palaces through which they passed. Some twenty natives, armed with poignards, brought up the rear.

Toki, a native who had grown old in the Viceroy's palace, led the way toward one of the ruined temples—that erected to Siva, the God of Destruction.

Lianor gazed with awed eyes at the magnificent palace, still bearing traces of former beauty.

"How wonderful! I must stay here, Leone, and sketch those old statues. We need go no farther. "

The day was beginning to get intensely hot, so the men were nothing loth to seek shelter in the cool temple, to sleep away the sunny hours.

Sketch-book in hand, the girl chose a shady retreat outside, and was soon lost in her work.

Presently the dreamy silence was broken; faint cries from afar reached her; and looking hastily up, Lianor saw a sight which made her stand rooted to the spot in speechless horror.

In the distance, pouring from out the mountains, were a multitude of Indians clad in divers costumes, carrying in their hands fantastic idols, and followed by a train of Brahmins, singing a low, monotonous chant, which had warned the girl of their approach.

Recovering her self-possession, and calling to the startled servants, Lianor entered the temple, where Panteleone and the men were quietly dozing.

"Leone, awake! The Indians are coming! "

The youth sprang to his feet, and, flinging one arm round his cousin, he drew a sharp poignard from his sash, and clutched it. firmly.

"Do not be afraid, Lianor. I will guard you with my life! " he said bravely.

"But is there no way to escape? " Lianor asked wildly, frightened at the peril into which her folly had brought them all.

"We might have gone; but it is too late. They are here, " Toki said gravely. "The only thing we can do is to hide amongst these broken statues, and perhaps we may be safe from their view, "

Scarcely had this been done than the procession arrived, stopped before the temple, and the men commenced building a huge square pile of wood; on this they placed a bier, on which lay the corpse of an old man, decked with silks and costly jewels.

Lianor and Panteleone, watching from their hiding-place the strange preparations, now saw a girl, very young and beautiful, but weeping bitterly, being dragged toward the pile by a tall, hard-looking woman.

"Come! " she cried, in loud, ringing tones, "now is the time to uphold the honor of your family, and show your courage! "

With a shudder the girl drew back, and clasping her hands piteously together, said:

"Why should I thus sacrifice my young life to the cruelty of your customs? I cannot endure the thought of being burnt alive—it is too horrible! "

"It is your duty! A widow must follow her husband in death, " coldly.

The youthful widow burst into passionate weeping, and gave an agonized glance around at the vindictive faces; not one among that multitude, she thought, felt pity for the girl who was condemned to so horrible a fate.

She was mistaken, and a second gaze revealed a young boy, not more than fifteen, who was quietly sobbing, an expression of deep anguish on his face.

"Satzavan, my poor brother, you also have come to witness my painful end! "

The boy went toward her, and wound his arms around her slim waist, drawing the dark head onto his shoulder.

"I would that I could help you, " he whispered. "But what can I do among all these fiends? "

"It is hard to die thus—so hard. "

"Savitre, I am more compassionate than you think, and I have here a draught which will send you into a deep sleep. The pain of death will thus be saved you, " Konmia broke in severely, holding a vessel toward the girl.

"No, no! " Savitre shrieked, pushing the potent drink away. "I cannot! Think how awful to awaken with the cruel flames wreathing round my body, and my cries for help useless, deadened by the yells of those people. I cannot—I will not die! "

Satzavan, deathly white, and with quivering features, drew her shuddering frame closer to him, and led her into the temple.

"Leave us for a moment, I implore you, " he said, turning to his aunt. "She loves me, and I may perhaps reconcile her to her fate. "

"You are the head of your family; I trust to you to bring her to reason—to save the honor of a name until now without blemish, " Konmia replied, and placing the poisonous flask in Satzavan's hand, she left them alone in the temple.

"Quick, Savitre; we will drink this draught together, and when they seek you, they will find us both cold in death. "

"You also, my brother, speak of death! I must escape—I cannot sacrifice my life! "

"Nor shall you, " a gentle voice broke in passionately, and Lianor, her face full of tender compassion, stood before the victim, Panteleone beside her.

"Follow me, " the latter said briefly, drawing the girl's arm through his. "Trust us, and you will yet be saved. "

With joyful hearts the two Indians accompanied their kind protectors, climbing among the broken gods, higher and higher, until they at last arrived without the temple, the other side from where the Indians were assembled.

There they were rejoined by the soldiers and attendants, and the little party commenced their homeward journey, hoping the wild group would not discover their presence.

But their hopes were not to be realized; ere they had gone many yards, the flight of the rajah's widow had been discovered, and with hideous cries they sought eagerly to find her.

It was not long ere they espied the small party, and full of triumph dashed toward them.

"Lianor, keep back—leave me to deal with these barbarians! " Panteleone said hurriedly, and in a minute a deadly fight began between the Indians and the soldiers.

But what was their strength against more than five hundred strong warriors? Ere long the brave party was captured, and while Konmia dragged the terrified girl towards the funereal-pile, the Indians shrieked aloud in triumphant gladness.

"To-morrow Siva will receive a sacrifice that will remain forever in the memory of those now living. To-day, our chief's widow; to-morrow, the Portuguese prisoners! "

****

After his daughter had gone, Don Garcia was filled with deep regret at having succumbed so readily to her wishes.

A presentiment of evil he could not control made him walk restlessly up and down the room.

A timid knock at the door roused him from his painful musings.

"Come in! " he cried quickly.

The door opened, and a tall, remarkably handsome man, dressed in the garb of a sea-captain, entered.

"What, Falcam, is it you, my boy? " the don cried gladly, wringing the young man's hand.

"Yes, senor. I have some papers from Tonza. There has been a slight rising at Diu, but, fortunately, we were able to suppress it in time, " handing the don a sealed packet.

After casting his eyes rapidly over the contents, Don Garcia smiled and turned with a pleased look towards the captain.

"Manuel tells me of your bravery in saving Diu, and asks me to promote you. I will do all I can. I am proud to call you friend. "

Luiz flushed, and a bashful light filled his eyes; but, ere he could answer, the don continued:

"However, you have come in time to be of service to me. My daughter, much against my wishes, has gone on an expedition to the Temple of Siva. From what I have since heard, I am afraid danger threatens my Lianor. Will you help me to rescue her? "

"Will I lay down my life to keep her from harm! Oh, senor, how can you ask? Let me start immediately, and ere long I will bring your child back in safety, " fervently.

Don Garcia was surprised at the young man's eagerness, but refrained from speaking, only to thank him for his kind offer.

Five minutes later Luiz Falcam, accompanied by a troop of brave sailors, started off towards the Temple of Siva.

As he neared, sounds of strife, mingled with heartrending shrieks, broke upon his ears. Urging his trusty band, he dashed onward until he arrived at the scene of terror.

Startled by the sudden apparition, the Indians lost, for a time, their self-control, and the sailors found it easy to subdue them.

Luiz had flown at once to Lianor's side, clasping her frail form tightly in his arms, while Panteleone wrenched Savitre from her aunt, as she was about to fling her on the now burning pile.

Even at the same moment, Satzavan, a smile of revengeful triumph on his face, wound a thick scarf over Konmia's head, and threw her with remorseless force into the flames, leaving her to meet the fate destined for his sister.

Those Indians who had not been taken had fled; so the band was free to wend its way homeward, though nearly half had been killed in the strife.

Still holding Lianor, now weeping quietly, in his arms, Luiz led the way towards the road, where the palanquin stood, and placing the girl gently in, raised her white hands passionately to his lips.

"Lianor, Lianor, my own darling! " he murmured, gazing into her pallid face with lovelit eyes. "If I had been too late, and found you gone! "

Lianor smiled tremulously through her tears, and a blush mantled to her cheeks.

"You have saved my life. I can never repay you, " earnestly.

Panteleone, still pale and anxious, now appeared leading the little widow, who seemed overjoyed at her release. She sank down gladly beside Lianor, and then the palanquin was borne away, guarded by Luiz and Panteleone, Satzavan walking behind.

Don Garcia's delight knew no bounds when he saw the procession entering the palace gates, and he ran eagerly to receive his daughter.

"My loved child! How unwise I was to let you go, to send you into danger, " he cried, carrying her in his arms from the palanquin to the marble hall. "If it had not been for our young friend, Falcam, I should never have seen you again. "

"But, papa, think! If we had not gone, this poor girl would have been burnt to death, " Lianor said, shudderingly, drawing Savitre towards her.

"Ah, yes. Poor child! " stroking the young widow's glossy black hair. "Now tell me all about it. " "Not yet, papa. Let us go and arrange our dresses; mine is torn completely to pieces, " laughingly holding up a fragment of cashmere, which in the struggle had become torn.

Holding Savitre's hand in hers, Lianor went swiftly to her rooms, where they could bathe their weary limbs in cool water, and change their tattered robes.

CHAPTER II.

Don Garcia was sitting in his study, regarding with some anxiety Luiz Falcam, who, tall and handsome, stood before him.

"You wish to ask me something, is it not so? Well, speak out, and be sure if it is in my power I will grant it. "

"I hardly like to ask. It is, I know, daring. I am but a captain, and you are one of the wealthiest men in India; yet I love your daughter, and that is what I wished to tell you, " earnestly.

Don Garcia smiled indulgently, and he gazed kindly at the young fellow's flushed face.

"I told you I would give you what you wished, and I will not break my word. I could safely trust Lianor to you. No other man I know has won so large a place in my esteem. But I dare not speak until I know what my daughter thinks. She will answer for herself touching so delicate a subject. Tell Donna Lianor to come here, " he said to Toki.

After what seemed an anxious age to poor Luiz, Lianor entered, leaning lightly on Savitre, somewhat astonished.

"Lianor, may I speak before Savitre? " the don asked gravely.

"Of course, papa. I have no secrets from her. "

"My child, " drawing her nearer to him, "Luiz Falcam has asked your hand in marriage; what answer shall I give him? "

Lianor blushed divinely, and her dark eyes shyly drooped before the eager glance from those loving blue ones fixed upon her.

"He saved my life, father. I will give it gladly to him, " she murmured.

"You love him, child? "

"Dearly. I shall be proud and happy to become the wife of Luiz, " gaining courage.

"You have my answer, Falcam. May you be content always. I give her to you with pleasure. "

In spite of the don's presence and Savitre's, Luiz could not refrain from drawing the girl into his arms and pressing fervent kisses on her smooth brow, and soft cheeks.

"You shall never repent your choice, darling, " he said tenderly. "I cannot give you wealth, but a true heart and a brave hand are solely yours, now and till death! "

"I know, Luiz dear, and to me that gift is more precious than the costliest jewels, " the girl whispered fondly.

Their happiness was not without its clouds; Luiz was compelled to leave his betrothed to guard a fort some distance away.

"I will return soon, dearest, " he said lovingly, holding the trembling girl in his strong arms, "and then your father has promised our marriage shall take place. "

"And you will not run into danger, for my sake? " Lianor pleaded, winding her white arms round his neck. "Think how desolate I should be without you! "

Don Garcia, having a great liking for the young man, saw him go with some regret.

"Don't stay away longer than you can help, " he said kindly. "God keep you, my boy. "

So Luiz parted from his love, and returned to Diu, carrying in his heart a cherished memory of Lianor, and a tiny miniature of her in his breast-pocket.

When he arrived at the governor's palace, he went directly to Manuel Tonza, to inform him of his departure.

The governor, a tall, dark-looking man of more than thirty, bore on his fine features a look of haughty sternness, mingled with some cruelty.

He glanced coldly at the young captain, and listened in silence to his explanations; but, as Luiz drew from his breast a sealed packet, given him by Don Garcia, Lianor's miniature fell with a crash to the ground, the jeweled case flying open.

Manuel picked it up from the floor with sudden swiftness, and gazed admiringly at the pictured face.

"Who is this? " he asked abruptly.

"Lianor de Sa, Don Garcia's daughter.

"Lianor de Sa, and so beautiful as this! " the governor muttered inaudibly. "I forgot she had grown from a child to a woman; I must see her. How comes 'it, though, her miniature is in his hands? Surely they could not have betrothed her to a captain! "

With a gesture of disdain he flung the miniature on the table, and told Luiz his presence was no longer needed.

Once alone, and a singular smile crossed the governor's face.

"I must pay Don Garcia a visit. It is long since I saw him. I never dreamt his little daughter had grown up so lovely. Thank Heaven, I am rich! My jewels and wealth might tempt a queen! I need not fear refusal from a viceroy's daughter. "

Full of complacent contentment, Tonza made hasty preparations for leaving Diu, and that same evening saw him a welcome guest of Don Garcia.

He was charmed with Lianor.

In spite of himself, a deep passionate love wakened in his heart for her, and he determined to win her for his wife.

First he wished to gain Don Garcia over to his side, so took an early opportunity of speaking to him on the subject.

The viceroy listened in grave silence, and a look of regret stole into his eyes.

"I am sorry, " he said gently. "Why have you come too late? My child is already betrothed. "

"To whom? " hoarsely.

"Luiz Falcam. "

"But he is only a captain, and poor! Surely you would not sacrifice your child to him? Think what riches I could lay at her feet! As my wife, Lianor would be one of the most envied of women. "

"I know, and I wish now I had not been so hasty; but Luiz saved her life, won my gratitude; then, as the price of his act, asked Lianor's hand. I was forced to consent, as I had said I would give him whatever he asked, " with a sigh.

"A promise gained like that is not binding. It was taking an unfair advantage of your gratitude. "

"I do not like to break my promise, but I will do what I can for you; I will ask Lianor, and if she cares for you more than for Luiz, she shall wed you. "

"Thank you; and I will try hard to gain her love, " Manuel answered hopefully.

When Lianor heard the subject of the conference between her father and Tonza, her indignation was unbounded.

"How can you act so dishonorably, papa? " she cried angrily, "after betrothing me to Luiz; now, because Tonza is rich and wishes to marry me, you would break your word. "

"But, my dear, think how different Manuel is to Falcam! He can give you a beautiful home, and jewels such as a queen might envy, while the captain can give you nothing. "

"He can give me a brave, loving heart, which is worth all the world to me! No; while Luiz lives I will be true to him. No other shall steal my love from him, " firmly.

"Is that the answer I am to give Tonza? "

"Yes. Thank him for the great honor he has done me; but, as I cannot marry two men, I choose the one I love—who first won my hand and saved my life. "

When Manuel heard her answer he was filled with rage and hate.

"So—so, " he muttered, a sinister look creeping over his face, "she will not wed me while Falcam lives. But should he die—what then? "

To Lianor he was always gentle, trying by soft words and many little attentions to win her regard; a very difficult task. Since her father's conversation, she shrank as much as possible from him, hoping he would understand her studied coldness.

"Savitre, " she said one evening, as they were dressing for a ball, given in her honor, "that horrid man's attentions are becoming intolerable! He will not see how I detest him, and am bound by love and promise to another. I wish Luiz was here; he has been away so long. I am tired of Tonza's persistence and papa's reproaches. "

"Never mind, dearest; all will be well when your brave lover returns. Perhaps he may be even now on the way. I am sure if he knew how terribly you were persecuted he would fly to you at once, " Savitre whispered softly.

"I feel miserable—unhappy. Lalli, put away those robes and give me a plain black dress. During Luiz's absence I will put on mourning, so Tonza can read the sorrow I feel in my heart. "

"But, dear, what will your father say? " Savitre asked anxiously.

"He will be angry, I know. But it is partly his fault I am obliged to act thus. "

In a few minutes Lalli and Tolla had silently arrayed their young mistress in trailing black robes, which clung softly to her beautiful form.

No jewelry relieved the somberness of her dress; her dark hair, thick and long, fell like a veil over her shoulders, adding to the mournfulness of her garb by its dusky waves.

Below, in the handsome marble hall, stood Don Garcia and Tonza, both watching with suppressed impatience the richly-hung staircase leading to Lianor's apartments.

"It is late. I hope nothing has occurred, " Manuel said anxiously, drawing the velvet curtain aside to gaze across the hall.

Even as he did so, Lianor, leaning lightly on Satzavan's shoulder, appeared, her graceful head held proudly erect, an expression of supreme indifference on her face.

Both men started with an exclamation of alarm—rage on Manuel's part.

"What! In mourning, and for a ball? " Manuel gasped with rising passion.

"Lianor, what does this farce mean? Why have you disguised yourself? How dare you disobey me when I said so particularly I wished you to appear at your best? I have been too weakly indulgent with you, and now you take advantage of my tenderness to disgrace me by showing my guests your foolish infatuation for a man to whom I now wish I had never promised your hand. "

Lianor lifted her reproachful eyes to his, her pale face, even whiter in contrast with her somber dress, full of resolute rebellion.

"I am not ungrateful, papa, for your kindness, but I will never forget the promise I gave Luiz. My love is not to be bought for gold; I gave it willingly to the man to whom you betrothed me, and, father, none of our family have ever acted dishonorably; so I am sure you will not be the first to break your word. "

"Do not be too sure of that, Lianor. I am more than half inclined to make you accept Tonza, and forget your vows were ever plighted to that pauper captain. "

"You could not be so hard, knowing how my happiness is bound up in him. I will never, while Luiz lives, give my hand to another. "

"Thank you, Lianor; nor will Falcam let you, " a deep voice broke in suddenly, and Luiz, his face flushed with mingled pleasure and disgust, came toward her, followed by his bosom friend, Diniz Sampayo, a young and rich noble.

Lianor threw herself into his arms with a glad cry, while Don Garcia and Manuel, full of rage, stole away, leaving the lovers alone.

"My darling, then I heard truly when they said my own dear love was being forced to wed another. Thank Heaven, I left Diu at once, and came to you, as your father seems inclined to listen to Manuel's suit, " Luiz said tenderly, bending to kiss the pale face.

"I am so glad you have come, Luiz! I felt so lonely without you near me, to give me hope and courage. "

"My poor little love! But why these robes, Lianor? I thought it was a day of festival at the palace? "

"I know; but I was determined, during your absence, to keep Tonza from paying me his odious attentions by putting on mourning. He could not fail to see where my thoughts were. Now you have returned, I will throw them aside, and show them it is a time of rejoicing with me. Wait, Luiz. "

With a tender smile the young lover unclasped her slender form and let her glide swiftly away.

But not long did he wait; soon the curtains were again lifted, and Lianor, radiant as a bright star, in trailing robes of white and gold, diamonds flashing on her bare arms and round her delicate throat, came towards him.

"My queen, my own dear love! what should I do if they took you from me? " passionately pressing her hands to his lips.

"They will never do that, Luiz. I am determined not to allow Tonza to win my father over to his way of thinking. "

Manuel Tonza watched the happy lovers with bitterest hate gnawing at his heart, deadly schemes against his fortunate rival flitting through his subtle brain.

Late that night, when the weary guests were parting, Tonza stole noiselessly from the palace; and when he returned, in less than half an hour, his face wore an expression of fiendish triumph and delight.

He was even polite to Luiz, much to that young man's surprise, though he doubted the sincerity of Manuel's words.

Happy and content, after a tender adieu to Lianor, the captain left the viceroy's palace, to seek his own apartments.

Not far had he gone, however, when a shadow stole silently behind him, and the next moment he felt himself suddenly grasped by powerful hands and flung to the ground.

Almost stunned by the fall, he was yet able to see the dark face bending over him.

From the shadows came another form, one he recognized. A gleaming poignard was placed in the assassin's hand, which descended ere he could break from that strong hold, and was buried deep in his heart.

Guiltily two forms glided away in opposite directions, leaving Luiz, pale and cold, lying in a stream of blood—dead!

* * * * * * * * * *

It was still early when Lianor awoke; but in spite of the drowsiness overpowering her, she hastily rose, and calling her maids, bade them quickly arrange her toilet.

"I am restless, and cannot stay longer indoors; I wish to be out in the fresh air, " she explained to Savitre, who entered soon after.

Scarcely, however, had they arrived without the palace gates, than Diniz Sampayo, his face pale and haggard, eyes full of fear and anguish, came hastily to her side.

"Donna Lianor, return to your father's house; I have something to tell you which I dare not breathe here—it is too horrible! Prepare yourself for a great shock, my poor child! I wish some one else had brought the awful tidings, " he cried hoarsely.

Lianor stood perfectly still, and her eyes grew wide and her face blanched with awakened fear. Clasping her hands piteously together, she said:

"Tell me now. I am brave — can bear anything! Is it Luiz? Is he ill — in danger? Oh, Diniz, for pity's sake tell me! "

Diniz took the trembling hands in his, and quietly bidding the others follow, led her silently through the town, until they arrived at the house where Luiz had taken rooms with his friend.

"Perhaps it is best you should see him. Poor Luiz! How can I break the awful truth to you? Your betrothed — the man you loved — is dead — murdered by a cowardly hand on his way home from your father's palace! "

Lianor grew deathly pale.

"Dead! " she repeated, clasping her hands despairingly to her throbbing brow. "It cannot be true! My darling dead — murdered! "

"My poor child, it is only too true! This morning he was found, and brought home, stabbed through the heart! "

"But who could have done it? " Savitre asked in a low, hushed whisper.

"I wish I knew. But, alas! that is a mystery! "

Lianor gazed helplessly from one to the other, then, breaking from her friend's gentle hold, staggered forward.

"Where are you going, Lianor? " Diniz asked, anxiously.

"To him. I must see for myself the terrible truth. "

"Can you bear it? "

"Yes — oh, yes! "

Very tenderly Diniz took one of the trembling hands in his, and led her toward a darkened chamber, where, on the blue-draped bed, lay the still form of his young friend.

A convulsive shudder shook Lianor's slender frame as she gazed on those handsome features set in death's awful calm; the closed eyes, which would never look into her own again; the cold lips which would never breathe loving words into her ear, or press her brow in fond affection

She could not weep, as Savitre wept; tears refused to ease the burning pain at her heart. Only a low moan broke from her as she threw herself suddenly over that loved body.

"My love—my darling! Why did I ever let you leave me? How can I live without you? "

"Hush, Lianor! Come, you can do nothing here. But one thing I promise you, I will avenge his death at any cost! The murderer will be found and punished—no matter who it is! " Diniz cried, earnestly.

"Thank you; and if I can aid, rely on my help, " Lianor murmured, bravely.

Then, bending reverently to press a last kiss on the pallid brow, she allowed Diniz to lead her from the room to her own home.

In the hall they were met by Don Garcia, in a terrible state of anxiety for his daughter.

"Where have you been, Lianor? What is the matter? You look ill! And what is that? " pointing to a vivid red stain which marred the white purity of her dress.

A low, delirious laugh broke from the girl's pale lips, and, stretching out her arms, she waved Don Garcia back.

"Do not touch me! " she cried, hoarsely. "He—my love, my darling—is dead! See, his life-blood stains my hands—my robe! Oh, heavens, that I should have lived to know such agony! "

She stopped; the outstretched arms fell inertly down, the graceful head drooped, and without one cry or moan, Lianor fell heavily to the ground—unconscious.

"Explain, Savitre—Sampayo, what means this strange raving? Who is dead? " Don Garcia said, fearfully.

"It means that Luiz Falcam was found murdered this morning! Your daughter went to see him for the last time, and returns, overcome with grief and sorrow. "

Without a word, but very white, the viceroy carried his child to her room, and left her in the care of Savitre and her two attendants, while he went to find the particulars of Falcam's tragic end.

For days and weeks Lianor kept to her rooms, seeing no one except her father and Sampayo, whom she looked upon as the avenger of Luiz.

Long and tenderly was her lover's memory sorrowed over, until the once beautiful girl was but a mere wraith.

A few weeks later Don Garcia himself was taken ill, and one day, feeling slightly better, he sent for his daughter, to whom he wished to speak on important business.

He was not kept long waiting. Lianor soon appeared, looking like a crushed flower in her somber robes.

"You wished to see me, papa? "

"Yes, Lianor; but you can almost guess for what. You know how much I desire to see you wedded to my friend; a man who loves you and will make you happy. I shall not live long, of that I feel sure. Manuel Tonza has waited patiently, and I think it is only right you give him hope. To-day you will accept his hand, and in another week, with my consent, you will become his wife. "

Lianor reeled against the bed, and held firmly to the silken curtains to prevent herself falling.

"Do you mean this, father? His wife—when he murdered Luiz? "

"What nonsense are you saying, child? Do not let me hear you speak like this again. What motive could a wealthy man like Tonza have in getting rid of one of his own employes? Grief has turned your brain.

Cast aside those weird garments, and in three hours be ready to receive your future husband. "

A low, gasping cry fell on his ears as he finished speaking, and he turned in time to see the slight figure sway to and fro, then fall heavily to the ground.

But what use was her feeble strength against the powerful wills of two determined men?

Ere the day was over, Lianor, with a heart full of bitter, despairing grief for Luiz, was bound by a sacred promise to a man whom she knew to be both bad and selfish—whom she hated!

CHAPTER III.

In one of the many straggling streets, almost hidden behind a few large shops of curious build, stood a small boutique full of ancient relics and jeweled bric-a-brac.

Inside, seated by the counter, writing in a large ledger, was an old man, whose hooked nose and piercing eyes proclaimed him at once to be from the tribe of Israel.

This Jew, Phenee, was not alone. Flitting about the shop, arranging the antique curiosities, was a young and very beautiful girl, with delicate features and lustrous, black eyes.

"Can I help you, grandfather? " the girl asked, suddenly stopping before the desk, and leaning both dimpled arms on the dusty book.

"No, no, Miriam; I have almost finished. Leave me for a few moments' quiet. "

Miriam sank gently on a high chair, and drooping her head pensively on her hand, sat for some time in unbroken silence, gazing out through the open door at the motley crowds passing by.

Suddenly a dusky form, clad in the garb of a fisherman, entered, and drawing near Phenee, glanced nervously around.

"I wish to sell that. How much will you give me for it? " laying a jeweled poignard, with a golden chain attached, on the desk.

Phenee took it up and examined it attentively, then looked searchingly at the man.

Satisfied at his scrutiny, the Jew named a very low price, one which his customer had some hesitation in accepting; but at last, seeing Phenee was obdurate, he took the offered money, and glided off like a spectre.

"What a curious poignard, and how pretty! " Miriam said, lifting it from the scales, where Phenee had placed it. "I am surprised he took so little for it. "

"I'm not. One can't offer too little for stolen goods. "

"Do you think this is stolen? "

"I am sure it is. That man never came honestly by it. "

Scarcely had the poignard been put on one side, when two young men, handsomely dressed, entered the shop, and asked for some emeralds.

"While you are choosing, I will have a look round at all these curiosities, Miguel, " the youngest of the men remarked.

"As you like; I shan't be long, Diniz. "

Sampayo nodded, and commenced his search, turning over every object that took his fancy, aided by Miriam.

"I will show you something very curious—a poignard strangely fashioned, " the girl said, drawing the weapon her grandfather had just bought from its hiding place.

Diniz took it up and examined it attentively, then a low cry broke from his lips, and his face grew pale.

"Where did you get this? "

"I have just bought it. It is a very pretty toy for a gentleman, " Phenee broke in persuasively.

With almost eager haste Diniz bargained for the poignard, and at last managed to bring the Jew down to ten times the sum he had given the fisherman.

After his friend, Miguel Reale, had chosen the jewels he wanted, Diniz hurried him away.

Not many hours later, as the young Jewess sat alone, her grandfather having gone some distance off on business, she was startled by Sampayo suddenly reappearing, a look of intense anxiety on his face.

"Senora, " he said politely, drawing from his breast the poignard, "can you tell me from whom your father bought this? "

"I do not know his name, but I believe he is a fisherman and lives in yonder village, " Miriam answered simply.

"Should you know him again? Pardon my asking, but it is very important I should discover the owner of this weapon. By doing so I may be able to bring a murderer to meet his doom, and avenge the death of my best friend! "

Miriam gazed at him compassionately, a serious light in her dark eyes.

"I will help you, " she said suddenly, moved as it were by a strange impulse; "I have long wished for occupation—some useful work, though I should have liked something less terrible than helping to trace a murderer; still, I will aid you if I can. "

"Thank you. But if he never came here again? "

"I shall not wait for that. To-morrow I will visit those huts in which the fishermen dwell; I may then find the man who sold the poignard, or at least a clew to the mystery. "

Diniz took one of the small hands in his, and pressed it reverently to his lips.

"You will not go alone; I will be your companion. Together we shall work better. But your father will he consent to your accompanying me? "

"My grandfather loves me too dearly, and trusts me too fully, to refuse me anything. He need not know the errand upon which I am bent, " a faint blush rising to her cheeks.

After making all necessary arrangements for the next day, Sampayo left the Jewess, to wait impatiently until the hour arrived for him to start on his melancholy errand.

It was still early when he left the crowed streets, to walk quickly in the direction of a small fishing village, some distance off.

Half way he saw the tall, graceful figure of a young girl, whose long veil of soft silky gauze hid her face from passers-by. He recognized her at once—it was the beautiful Jewess. So, hastening his steps, he soon stood before her.

"Senora, " he said gently.

The girl started, turned, then smiled through the screening folds of gray.

"It is you? I was afraid you would not come, " in a relieved tone.

"I am too anxious to find that man, to lose the chance you have so kindly given me. I only hope I am not putting you to any inconvenience, " Diniz said, gallantly.

"Not at all. I am only too happy to be of some use, " earnestly.

For many hours they wandered about from house to house, Miriam having armed herself with a large sum of money, hoping by acts of charity to gain access into the poor dwellings.

They were almost despairing of finding a clew to the whereabouts of the fisherman, when three little children, poor and hungry-looking, playing outside a tiny hut, attracted Miriam's attention.

Stooping, she spoke gently to the little things, and won from them the tale of their excessive poverty, which she promised to relieve if they would take her to their mother.

This they willingly did, and Miriam found a pale, delicate-looking woman, who, notwithstanding the raggedness of her dress, still bore traces of having been at one time different to a poor fisherman's wife.

Encouraged by the soft tones of her mysterious visitor, the woman gradually unburdened her troubled heart by telling her the history of her wretched life; how she had been doomed to follow her husband, an Indian chief, to death; but, loving life better, she escaped with her little children, but would have died of hunger on the seashore if Jarima, her second husband, had not rescued her and offered her his name and home.

"He is very good to me and my children; the past seems but a dream now. If only we had money, all would be well. "

Miriam, with a few gentle, consoling words, slipped a few bright coins into the tiny brown hands of the astonished babies; then, with a sigh, she bade the grateful mother adieu and went out to where Diniz was waiting.

He read by her face that she had no better tidings, and, drawing her hand through his arm, he turned away.

"Will it never come—the proof I want? " he said, half bitterly.

Scarcely had the words left his lips when a glad cry of "Father! " rent the air, and three small forms bounded over the white shingle towards a tall man, dressed in white linen.

Almost convulsively Miriam pressed Sampayo's arm to arrest his hasty steps.

"We need go no farther, " she whispered. "That is the man you want; and if he is that woman's husband, his name is Jarima. "

"Thank Heaven! To-morrow he will be arrested and the truth discovered, " Diniz muttered.

Silently they watched the man walk towards his humble home, the children clinging lovingly to his hands. The woman came forward with a bright smile, holding up her face to receive his caress.

"There can be no doubt. It is Jarima, and the man who sold the poignard. "

"Luiz's murderer, " Dinis added between his set teeth.

Almost feverishly Sampayo hurried Miriam away. He was anxious to tell Lianor of his success, and bring the assassin to justice.

Some distance from the Jew's shop he bade Miriam adieu, promising to call and let her know the result.

On reaching Don Garcia's palace Diniz was surprised at the sounds of bright music, mingled with happy voices, that floated on the air.

Satzavan was the first to meet him, and he went forward with a welcoming smile.

"Where is Lianor? " Diniz asked anxiously, glancing round the deserted halls.

"In the grounds. Don Garcia has his home full of guests in honor of his daughter's betrothal with Manuel Tonza. "

"Lianor betrothed, and to him! " in consternation.

"Yes, " sadly; "her father has commanded her to accept him, and, since she lost poor Falcam, she is indifferent whom she weds. "

"But Tonza above all other men! " bitterly.

With a dark shadow on his brow, Diniz followed the young Indian into the spacious grounds, where Lianor, surrounded by many richly-dressed ladies, was sitting.

"I cannot speak to her before all those people. Go, Satzavan, and bring her to me. "

The youth darted off obediently, and presently returned to the tree where Diniz stood almost hidden by its shady branches, leading Lianor, whose face wore a look of some wonder.

"Diniz, is it really you? Have you brought me any news? " she asked eagerly.

Sampayo took her outstretched hand and kissed it reverently.

"Yes, " he said softly; "good news. "

"What is it? Tell me! "

"I have discovered the man who, I think, struck the blow by instigation of the real murderer. Until he is taken I can do nothing further. "

"But who is he? How did you find him? "

"He is a poor fisherman, named Jarima, and it was through a young Jewess, Phenee's grandchild, to whom the poignard was sold, I found him. "

199

"That was very good of her to help you. "

"It was, indeed. The whole morning she has searched with me for the man, and at last our labor was rewarded. To-morrow Jarima will be under arrest. "

As the words left his lips, a sudden movement amongst the trees startled them.

"I am sure that was some one, " Lianor cried, turning pale, and clasping Diniz's arm.

Satzavan glided noiselessly away, but soon returned to say no one had passed by.

Possibly the noise was occasioned by the wind rustling through the leaves.

"Very likely, " Lianor said quietly, "though it made me nervous. Suppose any one overheard us? "

"Rest assured, dear, that nothing now can come between me and my revenge. But, Lianor, is it true you are betrothed to Tonza? "

"Yes, Diniz, it is true. Papa has commanded me to accept him. I hate him; but now poor Luiz is dead, I care not who becomes my husband, " hopelessly.

"I wish it were other than Tonza, Lianor. I cannot trust him; nor will I believe but what he had a hand in Luiz's death. "

"That is what I think, but papa says it is only fancy; Manuel is too upright to do such a treacherous thing. "

A silvery laugh broke suddenly on the silence which had fallen between them, and Savitre, leaning lightly on Panteleone's arm, stood before them.

The rajah's young widow made a strange contrast to Lianor, gay with rich colors.

Judging from Panteleone's ardent gaze, he, at least, saw some beauty in the dusky, changing face.

"What, Sampayo! I did not know you were here, " the young man cried gladly, seizing Diniz's hand in a warm grip. "Have you brought good news? "

"Yes, better than I expected, " Diniz answered; and briefly recounted the success which had attended his morning's search.

"I do not wish to meet your father to-night, Lianor; until this business is settled, I could not enter into any amusement. First, I will go to Henrique Ferriera, the magistrate, and arrange with him about Jarima's capture. "

"But you will come to-morrow, will you not—to tell me the result? " Lianor asked anxiously.

"Assuredly; unless anything serious prevents me. "

"Thank you, " she murmured gratefully.

A kind hand-pressure from all, and Sampayo walked quickly away; while Lianor, her heart somewhat lightened by this news, returned to her father's guests with Satzavan.

Savitre would have followed, but Panteleone held her back with a few whispered words, and, nothing loth, the little widow sauntered with him through the shady grounds, apart from the rest.

"Savitre, " Leone said suddenly, "would you be willing to leave your country—to go with me to Portugal? "

Savitre gazed at him in some wonderment.

"Surely you are not thinking of leaving India? " she cried, a sudden anxiety dawning in her dark eyes.

"Yes; my father wishes me to return, and as soon as Lianor is married we are going. "

The girl remained silent; only a few pearly tears rolled down her cheeks.

"Savitre, dearest one, do not weep! Would it be so dreadful for you to quit the country? "

"It is not that, " with a stifled sob; "but I had not thought of your leaving us, or the friendship between us being broken. "

"Nor will it, my darling! Don't you understand? I love you too dearly to give you up; I want you to be my wife, so that none can part us. Say my hopes are not all in vain! "

A vivid flush mantled the clear, dark skin, and the lustrous eyes drooped in confusion.

"You really mean that? You love me, a girl who is not even of your own kind? "

"I love you with all my heart and soul. Ever since the day when It drew you half-fainting from off the already lighted pile, I have felt my affection growing deeper and deeper, until it has absorbed my whole being. My happiness is never complete unless I am near you. Tell me, darling, that you return my love! " "How could I help but love you—you who saved my life? Oh, Leone, you cannot think how proud I am at being chosen by you before all others! "

With a joyous exclamation, Panteleone drew her to his breast, pressing passionate kisses on her brow, cheeks, and lips, his heart thrilling with rapture at the realization of his dreams.

CHAPTER IV.

The next morning a small band of soldiers, headed by Henrique Ferriera, wound their way toward the humble home of Jarima.

On arriving, they found to their astonishment the door fastened close, and no one to answer their knock.

"Never mind, break it down, " Henrique said, roughly.

In obedience a few heavy blows fell on the woodwork, which soon gave way beneath their force.

Stepping over the scattered splinters, Henrique saw a sight which filled him with horror.

Crouching on the bare floor, her hands twined convulsively in her long hair, was a woman, with three sleeping children leaning against her.

On a hard straw mattress, almost in shadow, lay Jarima, his face covered with blood, which oozed in streams from his mouth.

Henrique gazed for an instant on the awful sight, then turned towards his men.

"We have arrived a little too late; blind men cannot see, or dumb ones tell tales. Some horrible wretch has done this deed, fearful of his betraying them. I wonder who? "

The woman, when questioned, could tell them nothing. She only knew her husband had been brought home in his present condition at daybreak, and remained unconscious since.

"I regret to say it is our painful duty to take him; every care will be given him. He is suspected of having murdered Luiz Falcam. "

"No, no; you are mistaken! It is some one else, not he. Jarima was much too gentle to kill any one! " the woman cried, passionately.

Her prayers and supplications were unavailing. Henrique was obliged to do his duty, and bade his men take the suffering man to prison.

Some hours later, as Diniz stood in his room, just before setting out in search of Henrique, that man entered the house, followed by several soldiers.

"Diniz Sampayo, I arrest you on the charge of having stolen a poignard, set with jewels, from Manuel Tonza de Sepulveda. "

Diniz started, and flushed angrily.

"I steal? When you know it is the weapon I bought from Phenee, the Jew, as proof against the murderer. "

"So you said; but we have heard another tale to that. Anyhow, if you are innocent, you will be set free as soon as you are tried. "

"But the man Jarima? Have you not been for him? "

"Yes, but he is useless; when we arrived, some one had been before us, and not only blinded him, but cut out his tongue, so that he could not speak. "

"How horrible! How could any one have been so cold-blooded? " Diniz gasped, turning pale.

"Evidently it was done for some purpose. But come, Sampayo, I cannot wait here. "

"Will nothing I say convince you I am innocent? If innocence gives strength, I shall soon be at liberty. "

Henrique smiled scornfully, and hurried the young man away.

"You will not be alone; your prison-cell is shared by another—Phenee, the Jew. An old friend of yours, is he not? " Henrique asked.

"Friend—no! I have only spoken to him once in my life. What is he arrested for? "

"Being a receiver of stolen goods, " grimly.

Diniz thought suddenly of Miriam, and wondered how she would bear this blow. Her only relative and dearly-loved parent torn from her side, to linger in a damp cell. How bitterly he blamed himself for having been the cause of Phenee's capture! If he had not disclosed the secret of Phenee having bought the poignard from Jarima, no one would have suspected him.

"Poor girl! She will regret now having helped a stranger, who, in return, has brought her only grief and desolation, " he murmured, sorrowfully.

Miriam passed nearly three days in sad thought, when her solitary mourning was broken by the visit of a thickly-veiled woman, whose low, sweet tones fell like softest music on Miriam's ear.

"Are you alone? " she asked, glancing questioningly round the room.

"Yes. Did you want me? "

"I do, very badly. I remembered only to-day that you once proved a true friend to Diniz Sampayo, and I came to know if you would again aid him? " throwing back her veil, and disclosing a pale, sweet face, stamped by deepest grief.

"Diniz Sampayo! But is he, then, in need of help—in danger? " a sudden fear lighting up her face.

"Yes, he is in prison, " sadly.

"You are sure? How can it be possible? What has he done? " in amazed wonder.

"He has done nothing. Only his enemies have thrown the suspicion of his having stolen a poignard from Manuel Tonza—a poignard which I know he bought here. It is my fault this has happened. It was to avenge the death of the man I loved—his dearest friend—that he placed his life in peril! "

"I remember well. It is quite true he bought it here, soon after Jarima, the fisherman, had sold it to my grandfather. He, poor dear, is also in sorrow, imprisoned for having received stolen goods, as if he could tell when things are stolen! " indignantly.

"I am very sorry, Miriam; but if you help me, you will help your grandfather also, " Lianor urged gently.

"I will! " Miriam cried firmly; "I will never give up until I have them both safely outside that odious prison! "

Lianor gazed with grateful affection at the girl's expressive face, which now wore such a look of determined courage.

"If I can do anything, let me know directly, " Lianor said, gently. "Gold may perhaps be useful, and I have much. "

"Thank you, but I am rich; and I know grandfather would lose all, rather than his liberty. You are Don Garcia's daughter, are you not? "

"Yes, " somewhat sadly. "You know me? "

"By sight, yes. "

"I shall see you again, I hope, " Lianor said, as Miriam followed her to the door. "You will tell me of your success or failure? "

"Yes; I will come or write. "

When her charming visitor had gone, Miriam returned to her seat, a pained expression on her bright face.

"He also there. Poor Diniz! But I will save him yet, " determinedly.

Hastily opening a heavy iron box, she drew out a handful of gold.

Placing this in her pocket, she softly left the house, and scarcely knowing what instinct prompted her, she hurried towards a small hotel not far from the sea.

"Can you tell me, " she began breathlessly to a sunburnt man standing near, "if there are any ships leaving here to-morrow? "

"I don't know, senora. I will inquire, " he answered politely, and after an absence of about ten minutes, he returned to say "that Captain Moriz, of the Eagle, was even then preparing for departure on the morrow. "

"Where does he live? " Miriam said, eagerly.

"He is staying at this hotel at present. "

"Do you think I could see him? It is very important "

"I dare say. You can at least try, " smilingly.

The Jewess thanked her good-natured commissioner, and lightly ascended the steps.

"I wish to see Captain Moriz. Is he in? "

"I think so, " the man answered after one quick glance at Miriam; "I will inquire. "

Miriam waited with growing impatience until the man returned, and was relieved when she heard that the captain was not only there, but would see her.

With wildly beating heart the girl followed her conductor to a large, darkly-furnished room, where, by a table scattered with papers, sat a tall, bronzed seaman.

"I believe you are leaving India to-morrow? Would you mind telling me where you are going? "

"To Africa, " a look of surprise crossing his face.

"Are you going to take passengers? "

"That was not my intention. "

"But if any one asked you, would you refuse? "

"I don't know. I did not want any one on board, " Moriz answered uneasily.

"If you knew it would do some one a great service? l am rich, and would pay you well; so do not hesitate on that account. "

"Is it you who wish to go? "

Miriam blushed, and bit her lip angrily. She had not intended to betray her secret so soon.

"Yes, it is I, and two other people. Will you take us, and set us down on one of those small islands on the coast, where no one would find us? "

Moriz hesitated; but he could not withstand the eager pleading in the slumbrous eyes, the intense pathos in the sweet voice.

"Yes, " he said at last, very slowly, "I will take you on board; but you must be ready by to-morrow night. I cannot wait for stragglers, " trying to force much severity into his tones.

"Oh, thank you! I am content now. Do not fear; we shall be in time. Until then adieu, " she said softly.

And, with a graceful bow, she departed.

Her next step was in the direction where Phenee was confined.

She found no difficulty in finding the jailer, a hard-looking man enough, though Miriam thought she could see a gentle expression in his eyes when they rested on two young children, whose pale, wasted features gave evidence of close confinement in that dreary place.

"I may win him yet by those little ones, " she murmured; "gold will have power to touch his heart for their sakes. "

"You wished to see me, senora? "

"Yes. I want you to answer a few questions. First, have you not got Phenee, the Jew, and Diniz Sampayo here? "

"Yes, senora. "

"Are they together? "

"No, senora. "

"Could it be possible for you to set them free, without fear of detection? " eagerly.

"Yes, senora; but I am not a traitor. "

"But think, Vincent: my poor grandfather has done no harm, and he will perish in that horrible place, though innocent. And the Senor Sampayo, as I have proof, bought the poignard himself from my grandfather. Why, then, should you say he stole it? " indignantly.

"It is not I who accused him; my duty here is to guard the prisoners— not to try them. "

"Vincent, " Miriam continued, in a low, pleading voice, "you are poor; your little children are pining for want of fresh, pure air. I am rich, and can give you enough money to live in comfort away from this close den. Release my friends, and the power of saving your children shall be yours. Look! " drawing one of the wondering girls to her side, "see how pale and thin she is! Can you refuse my offer when the lives of those you love depend upon it? "

Vincent felt the truth of her words, and knew the only things he cherished on earth, those innocent children, were slowly fading and pining away for want of fresh air.

The man raised his head, and glanced earnestly at the moved expressive face, then in a low, hoarse voice he muttered:

"Be it so. I will help the prisoners to escape. I cannot see my little ones dying before my eyes, when an opportunity is given me to save them. "

"Then to-morrow at sunset you will bring them to the Golden Lion, I will be there, ready with the money. "

"I will not fail, senora. May Heaven forgive me if I am doing wrong!"

After a few instructions, the happy girl went swiftly away, but ere she had moved far, she returned, and paused before Vincent.

"I forgot to ask you about that poor man, Jarima, " she said, gravely.

"He did not live long, senora, after he was brought here. "

"And his wife—children? "

"Of them I know nothing, " he answered quietly.

Ere she continued her homeward way, Miriam sped swiftly toward Jarima's poor home, and knocked gently at the door. It was opened by the eldest of the three children, and forcing a purse of money into his brown hand, the girl whispered sweetly:

"For your mother, little one; from a friend, " then moved silently away, hurrying homeward to await patiently for the long hours to pass, ere her grandfather would be released.

Vincent, true to his word, gathered his few belongings together, and when the evening came, went softly to the cells in which his prisoners lay, and, setting them free, told them to follow him.

Wondering, yet glad, Phenee, leaning on Diniz's arm for support, slowly obeyed the jailer, who, accompanied by his two children, led them toward the hotel Miriam had named.

There, sure enough, the young Jewess was waiting, and after tenderly embracing Phenee, and smiling softly at Diniz, she turned to Vincent and placed a bag of gold in his hand.

"This is your reward. May you and your little ones live in happiness! " she said earnestly.

"We leave Goa to-night, senora. My life would be worth nothing if I stayed here after this. Good-by, and thank you for your generosity. "

Miriam hastened her grandfather to the ship, shocked at his feebleness; but for Sampayo he would scarcely have been able to get there.

Only once he spoke to the girl ere he retired to his cabin for the night.

"The money and jewels, Miriam — what have you done with them? "

"They are here, grandfather. I brought everything of value away with me. "

"That is right, child. You are a good girl! "

Miriam stood rather sadly beside the bulwarks, gazing at the land in which she had been born, and which she was now leaving forever.

A low sigh broke from her lips.

"Why do you sigh? Are you sorry to quit your native land? " a voice whispered in her ear.

"Yes; though for my grandfather's sake I cannot deeply regret it, " Miriam answered, gazing at Diniz with tear-dimmed eyes.

"I have not thanked you yet for having released me from that dreadful place, or even a worse doom. I am still scarcely able to realize my good fortune. What made you, a stranger, think of one whom all others had forgotten? "

"Not all. It was Donna Lianor who told me where you were, and asked me to help you, " Miriam said, blushing beneath his tender, grateful gaze. Besides, I looked upon you as a friend, " almost inaudibly.

"That is what I want to be—your friend. And Lianor—how is she? — well? "

"As well as it is possible to be under the heavy trial she went through this morning. She was married to Manuel Tonza, " sadly.

"Poor girl! Poor Lianor! Hers is indeed an unhappy lot! " Diniz murmured pityingly.

CHAPTER V.

In a large, handsome room, overlooking a shining river, now ablaze with sunshine, sat a beautiful woman, wearing on her face unmistakable signs of sadness.

She scarcely heeded the opening door, until two pretty children came bounding to her side, clambering onto her chair and lap.

Then her face changed, and a sweet, tender smile chased away all gloom; the idle hands were busy now stroking the curly heads pressed so close against her.

"I would have brought them to you before, but their father wished to keep them; he is always so happy when they are near, " a little, dark-eyed woman, clad in picturesque robes of brilliant crimson and gold, said rapidly, as she threw herself down on a pile of soft cushions opposite the sweet, pale mother.

Lianor sighed, but she could not look sad long with those loved children clasped in her arms.

"I cannot understand Manuel, " she said, with a puzzled expression in her eyes; "he is so strange, sometimes gay—almost too gay; then he relapses into a gloomy, brooding apathy, from which even the children have no power to rouse him. "

"But you have. He is never too morose to have a smile for you. I think, sometimes, he feels lonely. You are bound to him, yet your heart is as unresponsive to his passionate love as if you were strangers, " Savitre said, thoughtfully.

"Do you think so, Savitre? I am indeed sorry; but you know how impossible it is to forget my first love. I like Manuel, but beyond that, affection—except for my darlings—is dead; buried in Luiz's grave. "

"Hush! here comes Manuel, " Savitre whispered, warningly.

It was indeed Manuel, older and graver-looking than of yore, with a deep melancholy in his eyes, brought there only by intense suffering.

Savitre, on his entrance, softly glided from the room, leaving husband and wife alone.

"Lianor, " he began, a bright smile lighting up his face as he bent to kiss her fair brow, "I have been thinking, and am resolved to quit India and return to Portugal. I have been here long enough. Don't you think that will be pleasant, dearest? "

"Nothing would please me more, " Lianor cried, delightedly. "The greatest wish of my life is to see Portugal once more, to show our country to our children, " bending to kiss her tiny daughter's face.

"Then it will be granted. Prepare to start as soon as possible. Now, I am determined to leave here. Something seems to urge me to go at once. "

Only too anxious, Lianor began her arrangements.

Savitre, who had never cared to leave her friend before, even to become Panteleone's bride, entered into the preparations with unconcealed eagerness.

She had faithfully promised her lover that, once in Portugal, she would, with his father's approval, marry him.

Lianor felt no regret at leaving India, except for a loved grave—her father's—which she had so carefully tended.

Not many days after, Manuel Tonza, his wife, children, Panteleone, and Savitre, accompanied by several faithful servants, including Lalli and Tolla, embarked in a fine stately ship, which was to bear them in safety to their home.

Tonza seemed full of joy as he saw the last lines of the Indian coast disappear. He had rarely appeared so happy since his marriage with Lianor five years before.

For several days the good ship went steadily on her way, until one night a terrific storm arose, and the vessel, heedless of the human cargo it was bearing, drifted onward at the mercy of the tempest.

Tonza, holding Lianor and his children closely to him, stood silently dismayed, scarcely able to realize the awful danger which lay before him and those he loved.

Still onward, through the almost impenetrable darkness, went the doomed ship, until, as the dense shadows began to clear and the storm to cease, a sudden shock was felt by all—she had struck against some rocks and was slowly sinking!

"We must be somewhere near land, " the captain cried, his voice sounding above the roaring waters.

By aid of the fast-breaking dawn, they could see the line of high, dark rocks, upon which the ship had met her fate.

With much difficulty and peril, under the captain's cool directions, the crew managed at last to leave the sinking vessel, not without much loss of life. Out of nearly five hundred only a few arrived in safety, amongst whom were Tonza, his wife, children, Savitre, and Panteleone.

When the day broke in calm splendor, the sun shown upon a mournful sight—a group of shipwrecked men and women.

No sign of habitation met their view; only a weary waste of bare land, sheltered by a few trees, from whose branches hung a goodly supply of fruit.

"If we go farther inland, we are sure to find some natives, if only savages, " Tonza remarked gravely; and followed by the men, he commenced the long, weary way.

Lianor, pale but firm, holding in her arms her little daughter, walked beside him, heedless of the fatigue which oppressed her and made her long to sink upon the sandy ground to rest.

Onward they went, never pausing to rest their tired feet until, as the day was about to decline, they came to a deep waterfall, over which they had to cross. No easy task, as the only means of doing so was by an uneven path, made from a line of rocks, on either side of which the boiling waters poured in terrific fury.

Tonza—who, now the captain had perished, placed himself at the head of the crew—was the first to put his foot upon the crossing; then, turning to the people, he said:

"Be careful, and not glance behind or down, or you will lose your balance and fall. "

Lianor, who, by her husband's wish, had given her child to one of the men, followed closely behind Manuel, who held his boy in his arms.

Silently, without daring to murmur one word, the men walked bravely onward.

They were nearly half way across.

Manuel had indeed touched firm ground, when a sudden cry from her little girl made Lianor turn in affright to see what ailed her.

That move was fatal; the next instant she had lost her footing and fallen into the dashing torrent.

With a despairing shriek Manuel stopped, and had not some one held him back, would have dashed in after his wife. Panteleone, who saw a chance of saving her, quickly slipped over the side, caught her in his aims as she was about to sink, then bore her to land.

Forgetful of all others, Manuel threw himself beside her still form, from which all life seemed to have fled, calling wildly on her name, pressing passionate kisses on her cold face, hoping by the warmth of his caresses to bring back the color to her cheeks.

But it was useless; Lianor was dead; her head having struck against a rock, caused instant unconsciousness, from which they could not rouse her.

When Tonza realized the awful truth he rose to his feet, pale and haggard, his eyes full of despairing anguish.

"It is just; my sin is punished. My wife, the only thing I loved on earth, for whose sake I committed crime, is taken from me! She alone had power to make me happy; without her I cannot live. It is time I confessed all, and you shall be my judges. It was I who caused the death of Luiz Falcam, that I might win his betrothed; and when I heard that Diniz Sampayo had discovered partly the truth, I had him thrown into prison on suspicion of having stolen the very poignard with which Luiz had met his death—one that I myself had placed in the assassin's hand! You all know how he escaped, but he is an exile for my fault. If ever you should see him, tell him his innocence is established; he can return to India in peace. You have heard my story, now judge me; " and with arms crossed over his breast, his head bowed in deepest grief and humility, he waited his sentence.

A dead hush fell over the group, broken only by the suppressed sobs of Savitre, who was crouching beside Lianor, and the pitiful moans of the little girl dying in one of the rough seamen's arms.

At last Pantaleone, a look of compassion on his face, went towards his friend, and, laying his head on Tonza's shoulder, said gently:

"My cousin, you have sinned, but God has sent your punishment; that is sufficient. Live to devote your life to bringing up the little motherless children left to you. Restore Sampayo to his own again; then try, by true repentance, to atone for the wrong you did him. "

Tonza raised his head, and glanced gratefully at Panteleone; but his eyes were full of firm resolution none could understand.

"You are good, but my life is worth nothing, now she has gone. See, this poor babe will soon follow her mother. Garcia I leave to you; he is too young to realize his loss; but never let him know his father's sin! " he exclaimed hoarsely; and, after pressing his boy tightly to his breast, kissed the dying child; then softly lifting Lianor in his arms, he first pressed his lips reverently on her pale brow, and, before any one could prevent him, or realize what he was about to do, he had sprang from the rock into the deep torrent, and disappeared with his precious burden from their view.

A cry of horror burst from the lips of all present, and many efforts were made to find their bodies; but in vain.

With saddened hearts the people turned away, and continued their journey, praying they might ere long find help and shelter.

Before the day had closed another soul had winged its flight to Heaven, and the tiny waxen form of Lianor's baby-girl left in its last resting-place in the golden sand.

A small wooden house, surrounded by sweet-scented flowers of brightest hue, amongst which a beautiful, dark-eyed woman was softly gliding, culling large clusters of the delicate blossoms.

As she stopped to gather a few rich carnations, singing in a low, musical voice, a man, young and handsome, slipped from beneath the pretty porch, and walking noiselessly behind her, suddenly lifted her in his strong arms, pressing the slight form tenderly to his breast.

"Take care, Diniz, " she cried, warningly, a ring of deepest joy thrilling her clear voice. "You will spoil all my flowers! "

"Except the fairest of all—yourself. Ah, Miriam, my darling! how happy we have been since that day when you so generously saved me from a felon's doom! " rapturously kissing the beautiful, dark face so near his own.

Their bliss was broken by a crowd of brown-skinned people, moving toward the cottage, seemingly acting under some emotion.

"What has happened? What is it? " husband and wife cried simultaneously.

"We have seen a party of white men, doubtlessly shipwrecked on the coast, coming in this direction. They are even now in sight, " one man said quickly,

Diniz flushed, and his eyes grew bright with suppressed joy.

"Perhaps some of our countrymen, Miriam. Let us hasten forward to welcome them, " he cried eagerly; and leading his wife, while the crowd followed curiously behind, Sampayo hurried in the direction from whence the strangers were coming.

It was not long before they met the tired crew, now dwindled to about twenty, many having perished on the way.

As Diniz stepped towards the first stranger, on whose arm leaned a young and beautiful woman, a low cry burst from his lips.

"Panteleone! " he gasped, "is it really you? "

"What, Diniz! " and the two friends, separated for so long a time, warmly clasped hands.

"But how comes it that you are like this? "

Panteleone briefly related their voyage from India, and the disastrous end. Tears shone in his eyes when he recounted the sad death of Lianor and her husband.

"Poor, poor girl! How sorry I am! " Diniz said mournfully, while Miriam, scarcely able to repress her sobs, drew Lianor's orphan boy in her arms, and bore him to their pretty home.

"You are welcome—all! " Sampayo said gently, turning to the haggard- looking seamen. "Come. "

A few days later a grand old ship, bound for Portugal, started from that coast, bearing the wrecked crew to their former destination.

Amongst those on board were Diniz and his wife (Phenee had long since joined his forefathers), who, now his innocence was made known, had no longer the fear of being imprisoned, and could return in safety to his native land.

Panteleone's father received Savitre with almost paternal love, and some months after their arrival, when their mourning for poor Lianor was lessened, the two faithful hearts became one.

Little Garcia, Tonza's son, was tenderly nurtured in their tranquil home, and the aunt he loved so dearly became a second mother, replacing the one he had lost.

No shadow of his father's sin darkened his young life; he lived unconscious of the sad fate of his mother, who, won by crime, by her death avenged Luiz Falcam, for, through her, Manuel Tonza had atoned for all.

THE END.

The latest Works of the most popular Authors.

HER FATAL SIN; A WOMAN'S LOVE; THE TRAGEDY OF REDMOUNT. by Mrs. M.E. Holmes.

BOUND BY A SPELL, by Hugh Conway

FORCED APART, OR EXILED BY FATE, by Morris Redwing.

DYKE DARREL, THE RAILROAD DETECTIVE; A LIFE FOR A LIFE, OR THE DETECTIVE'S TRIUMPH; $5000 REWARD; OR CORNERED AT LAST, by Frank Pinkerton.

HONOR BRIGHT, AND TWENTY CRUSOES, by Dwight Weldon.

A GOLDEN HEART, by Charlotte M. Braeme.

A HOUSE PARTY, by Ouida.

LADY VALWORTH'S DIAMONDS; MILDRED TREVANION, by the Duchess.

FOR SALE EVERYWHERE.

CPSIA information can be obtained
at www.ICGtesting.com
Printed in the USA
BVHW040707070223
657963BV00017B/112